THE ALPHA'S REDEMPTION

THE KINCAID WEREWOLVES #3

L.E. WILSON

le@lewilsonauthor.com

Print Edition - ISBN: 978-1-945499-48-7

Publication Date: March 23, 2018

Editor: Jinxie Gervasio @ jinxiesworld.com

Cover Design by Coffee and Characters

Cover Photo: Kruse Images and Photography

Cover Model: Scott Nova

On a cold, winter night,
When the wind gusts and the wolves sing,
Does their song call to the wildness in your soul?
Or will you run in fear?

L.E. Wilson

CHAPTER 1

With the tip of his index finger, Keegan McRae slid the silver links of the necklace—*her necklace*—around on the polished oak table, watching as the morning light glinted off the bright metal. A soft growl rumbled in his throat, and he flattened his palm over the chain.

Resting his palms on his jean-clad thighs, he closed his eyes and rolled his head on his shoulders, trying to ease the tension. Then, with a sigh, he picked up the chain and refastened it around his neck. The tree pendant settled just below the hollow of his throat.

It was unusually cool for this time of year in Texas, and Keegan picked up his coffee, automatically blowing on the surface to cool it off.

He wondered if the Seattle pack would agree to his terms.

He wondered if *she* would agree to them.

After what had happened to his own father at the

hands of a Fae—an obsession that had ended in his death —he wondered why he should even care.

Tilting the heavy mug up to his mouth, he took a good slurp. But as soon as the brew hit his tongue, he spit it back into his cup. The taste was bitter enough to make him pucker, and he craned his neck around, looking for Corrina. The only female in the pack, she was also the only one who could brew a decent pot of coffee.

But the kitchen was completely empty.

Removing his buckskin hat, he set it on the bench beside him and ran a hand through his hair. He needed a haircut.

Stone, his new second in command, closed the door to his room upstairs, and soon, the heavy tread of his boots thundered down the wood stairs. He pulled his shirt over his head as he descended and gave Keegan a grin, his teeth a shocking white in his ebony face.

"You look like you're having a bad mornin', boss."

"I'm looking for Cor. This coffee is downright awful."

"That's because Corrina didn't make it. She went on a run last night, and hasn't come back yet that I know of. Something must be stuck in her craw."

Keegan had a good idea what that "something" was— him. Or rather, what he was about to do. Corrina had been a part of his pack for a long time, was one of his father's pack before this, and normally they agreed on how he chose to run it. But during one of their nightly sit-downs on the back porch the previous evening, she'd made it quite clear she thought he was following in the footsteps of his father.

But that wasn't the case. He wasn't under some kind of

spell. It was just a normal, healthy attraction. An attraction he'd fought for as long as he could.

He picked up his buckskin hat from the table and slapped it onto his head. "Yeah, she's not real happy with me."

Stone grabbed the OJ out of the fridge and sat down across the table from him, not bothering with a glass. "Whadya do now?" Lifting the carton to his mouth, he chugged down some juice, then wiped his mouth with his sleeve.

Keegan raised one eyebrow as he watched him. "Speaking of Cor, don't let her catch you doing that. She'll skin you alive and use your hide for her new rug."

With another grin and a wink, Stone said, "She won't know, unless you rat me out."

Keegan indicated for him to carry on as he was before he picked up the conversation where they'd left off. "I'm putting myself at 'undo risk' according to her." He was careful to keep any emotion out of his tone. "Being led around by the wrong head." This time he allowed himself to smile. "And speaking of—" he waited until Stone stuck the container back in the fridge and returned to the table—"I'm gonna need you to come with me tomorrow."

"Sure. Where are we going?"

"To meet the Seattle pack."

Understanding dawned across Stone's face. "Ahh. So, that's what Corrina's pissed about." He rapped the table with one knuckle. "I have to tell ya, man, I'm in agreement with her on this here issue, especially after what happened the last time one of those shifters came to visit. I wasn't a fan of Jace, as you know, but I respected his position in this pack."

"Jace was an ass, and he got himself killed. I'm not holding that against Marc, or his pack. He was protecting his female. Any one of us would have done the same thing." Although not all of them did as good of a job at it.

Stone considered that for a second. "All right, then. All right. But what about the rest of it? What changed your mind? I thought you didn't want to agree to an alliance. Not until there was proof. Like the soul suckers actually knocking at our door." He paused, his sharp brown eyes penetrating Keegan's skull in that uncanny way he had. "Or is there something you need to tell me?" Before Keegan could answer, Stone's hackles rose, filling the air with tension. "Did you hear something? Is it true? The Dark Fae are coming?"

Keegan held up his hand, halting any more questions. "I don't know that for sure, yet."

"Then what's this meeting all about?"

Keegan saw no sense in beating around the bush. "Cedric Kincaid has something of mine, and I want it back." He took another sip of his coffee, grimaced, and gave it up. Getting up from the table, he took his mug over to the sink and rinsed it out before sticking it in the dishwasher. It took him a moment to notice the absolute silence in the room. Turning around, he found Stone staring at him with a strange expression on his face. "What?"

Stone cocked his head as he studied the Alpha. "You're going after her. The dark-haired one."

It wasn't a question, so Keegan saw no reason to respond.

Stone released a hard breath of air. "Are you sure you wanna go there, man?"

Keegan stilled, lowering his voice. "Go *where*, exactly, Stone?"

But Stone wasn't put off. "This is a mistake, Keegan. The pack will never accept our Alpha bringing one of *them* into the pack."

He didn't say it, but he didn't need to. Keegan could hear the implied *like your father did* loud and clear.

That, if nothing else, was enough to make up his mind. He was nothing like his father, and she was nothing like the freak of nature who'd seduced his sire into such madness his own son was the one who'd had to put him out of his misery.

The pack could accept it, or they could find themselves a new pack. Keegan took off his hat and ran his hand through his short hair before settling it back on his head. "Are you coming with me, or what?"

Stone grinned and got up from the table. "Oh, yeah. I'm coming."

"Good. Be ready by three a.m. We have a long drive ahead of us."

The sun was sinking low on the horizon when Keegan and Stone pulled off to the side of a rural road just outside of Las Vegas. The desert held little appeal for werewolves, what with their naturally higher body temperature, all the fur, and no shelter from the sun and heat and all, and as such was considered neutral ground for the two packs to meet. Flat, sandy terrain could be seen for miles in any direction. It was a good spot. Out in the open. No way for anyone, or anything, to sneak up on them.

Keegan and Stone waited beside Keegan's pickup, watching waves of heat rise from the asphalt as a cloud of dust rapidly approached from the northwest. The front end of a lone vehicle soon appeared. And inside that vehicle would be Cedric and Marc, from the Seattle pack. Keegan checked his phone. They were right on time.

"They'll never agree to this." Stone's low voice broke the tense silence.

"Yeah, they will." In spite of Keegan's confident tone, his nerves were shot. But he couldn't show it. He was an Alpha. Alphas needed to be in control. Always.

Nothing more was said as they waited for the others to reach them. It took quite a while longer than one would think; distance could be deceiving in the desert.

While he waited, Keegan wondered—and not for the first time—if Stone was right and he should just let this shit go.

But he couldn't let it go. He couldn't let *her* go.

A classic Chevy El Camino slowed down and came to a stop about twenty yards from where they stood. Black, with tinted windows, it was near impossible for the average human to see inside. The engine cut off and the driver's side door opened. A large male with slicked-back, dark hair unfolded himself from the seat. When he turned to close the door, Keegan saw his hair wasn't greased to his head, but pulled into a long, wavy ponytail. Ice-blue eyes caught and held his for a moment, and then the male gave a nod of greeting and strode forward.

He was big, this Alpha. Taller than Keegan, with about fifty extra pounds of muscle on him. But it wasn't his sheer size that made him so daunting, it was the Alpha in his aura. The dominant gene practically oozed from his pores. A wolf was either born with it, or he wasn't. And this male definitely had it.

Keegan could understand why he had the reputation he did.

The passenger side door opened, and Marc got out. He looked no different from when he'd been a guest at the ranch months ago, other than a bit of a softening around his eyes and mouth. Caused, no doubt, by the fact his female was safe back in Seattle and in his bed. The pup had some *cojones*, that was for sure, showing up here again after the stunt he'd pulled at the rodeo. He didn't fidget or look away, or otherwise act nervous in any way. No, he walked up and looked Keegan right in the eye, and he had to respect that about the male.

Keegan straightened as the Seattle pack leader approached and stuck out his hand. "Cedric Kincaid, Alpha o' th' Seattle pack." The Scottish brogue was heavy in his speech, even though Keegan knew he'd been in the States for a long time.

Keegan took his hand in a firm grip. "Keegan McRae."

They shook, and Cedric indicated Marc coming up on his right. "And ye ken Marc, here."

Keegan touched the brim of his hat. "Marc. How have you been?"

"Verra well, thank you." The words weren't spoken lightly.

"I appreciate ye meeting us like this," Cedric said. "And I would like tae apologize, sincerely, for all tha' happened while Marc was yer guest. It was no' his normal character tae cause such a commotion. I can trust him tae keep his wits aboot him, which is why I sent him tae ye when I couldn't come myself."

"I understand," Keegan said. *More than you know.* "Sometimes our wolf gets the better of us. Marc is an honest and upstanding guy, I knew that about him right away, which is why I didn't kill him."

Cedric pinned Keegan with those eerie eyes, and he

held his stare without flinching. It wasn't a challenge. More a show of mutual understanding and respect.

Marc stepped forward until he was shoulder to shoulder with Cedric. "I meant no disrespect tae ye, Keegan. Ye ken that. But I would do it all again in a heartbeat tae save my Bronaugh and her family." He glanced over at Cedric, and straightened his spine. "That being said, I will no' argue aboot any punishment ye deem necessary tae get us back on even footing."

Although he'd never doubted Marc's character, Keegan's respect for him grew a whole bunch right then and there. "That won't be necessary, Marc. Jace's death was unfortunate, but not a big surprise, to be honest. If it hadn't been you, it would've been someone else. He liked to rile up any wolf he felt was a threat, throw his weight around. It was one of the reasons I made him my second, to try to keep him out of trouble. However, Stone here"— he nodded at the male next to him—"always been my true right-hand man."

Comprehension crossed Marc's face. "Ach. Aye. That explains so much. I could no' understand why ye let him treat ye as ye did," he said to Stone.

"Just keeping the peace, Seattle. Or, trying to," Stone told him. "I have to admit, I don't agree with letting you off for killing one of our pack, but I will respect Keegan's decision about it."

Marc gave him a nod. "Thank ye."

Cedric put his large hand on Marc's shoulder, pride for his wolf written all over his face, then looked to Keegan. "Can we walk a bit?"

They fell into line—the two leaders walking side by

side, with Marc and Stone coming up behind them. Close enough to protect their Alphas if the need arose, but far enough back to give them a modicum of privacy.

"Thank ye, again, for agreeing tae meet with me," Cedric said. "And for yer leniency with Marc's offense."

Keegan knew better than to take the apology for anything other than what it was, a show of respect for a fellow Alpha. Cedric had no fear of him, of that he was absolutely certain. But he appreciated the olive branch. "It's all good between me and Seattle, Cedric, but I appreciate it. Now, why don't you catch me up on anything that's happened since the summer?"

"There's no' much tae tell on our side o' things. Tha' daft prince o' th' Fae has gone silent the past few months. It's verra strange. He was all up our arses, and then suddenly falls off th' face o' th' earth." Cedric shook his head. "I dinna ken if this is good news or bad."

"How is he taking the news of a soul sucker—uh, *an olc* —in his midst?" He corrected himself, but too late. Ah, well. Nothing he could do about it now. And it wasn't like Cedric didn't know the mate Marc had killed for was a Dark Fae.

Cedric gave him a sharp look, but then his features softened. "Ach. Aye. He had a wee bit o' fun with her at first but gave her back tae us unharmed. Dinna fash yerself, Keegan. We're keeping an eye on her." He glanced over his shoulder at Marc.

Keegan glanced back also, and Marc gave him an assertive nod of agreement. He turned back to Cedric. "But you still think there's a danger of the soul suckers getting out?"

"That's what I've been told," Cedric said. "But there's something else that's come tae my attention having Bronaugh and her family with us."

His tone caught Keegan's attention. "What would that be?"

Cedric stopped walking and turned to face him, and Keegan did the same.

"There are more o' th' dark ones running loose out there. Bronaugh says she kens o' at least fifty more, other than herself. Some out o' their minds with th' hunger, some no'."

"Doesn't surprise me," Keegan told him. "We had two of them locked in cells on my ranch."

"Aye. Marc told me."

Keegan heard the censor in his tone but chose not to challenge it. It would do no good. The soul suckers had provided months of entertainment before they finally gave in to their disease. A couple of his guys had found them dead in their cell just a week before. Others would think what they would of him and what he did to keep the peace, and there wasn't much he could do to make them understand. "So, what's your point here?"

"My point"—Cedric spit the word at him—"is ye ken how dangerous they are. There is no bringing them back, no helping them, in spite o' what some might say."

He mumbled that last bit so quietly, Keegan almost didn't catch it. "Anyone who thinks a soul sucker can be brought back to the living is two cans short of a six pack."

Cedric gave him a puzzled expression.

"Not all there," Keegan clarified.

"Ach. Aye. If ye ken this, I would like tae ask ye again

tae consider joining our packs together. As th' two most respected packs this side o' th' ocean, it would do a lot tae increase th' trust between everyone if we were united."

Keegan crossed his arms. This was exactly how he'd hoped the conversation would go, but he wasn't ready to show all of his cards just yet. "And how exactly would that work, Cedric? There can only be one Alpha. Will we fight to the death for the position? As our law dictates?"

But Cedric shook his head. "I ken that's how it's always been done, but in this situation, I thought we could try something a wee bit different. We would swear alliance tae each other, but otherwise, nothing else would change."

"My pack will obey no Alpha but me."

"Aye, th' same with mine. I've given this a lot o' thought." Cedric stepped closer, the passion he felt for his cause plain to see. "The packs will remain as they are. My wolves will answer only tae me, and yours tae ye, as it's always been. But they will swear an allegiance o' sorts tae th' other Alpha, and we—th' Alphas—will work together tae put a stop tae th' terror that's coming."

"Why do we need an alliance to do that? We could just agree to put aside the pissing contests that normally occur between two Alphas and work together. Fight together. Send those bastards back where they belong *together*."

"Aye, we could do that. But having a joining of our packs is th' only way tae ensure no one gets any flighty ideas. And it will ensure my wolves will follow ye if it comes tae that, and yours will follow me."

"And if you die in this supposed war?"

"Then I would ask ye tae take in my pack and make them a part o' yer own. And I will do th' same. With an alliance already between us, there'll be no hemmin' and hawin' aboot it, no arguing tha' could cost lives, and I willnae have tae worry tha' my pack is taken care o'."

Keegan had to admit, he made a compelling argument. And everything he said was true. A lot of lives were lost in the last war, needlessly, because of hot-blooded wolves not wanting to obey any other Alpha but their own. Not to mention all of the dick measuring that went on between the Alphas themselves.

He agreed with all of it. He had since Marc had first proposed the idea. But back then, something had held him back from jumping into this deal. An opportunity he wasn't even aware of at the time, but one he intended to take full advantage of now. "All right. I'll agree to your alliance." He held up a hand as Cedric breathed a sigh of relief. "But on one condition."

Cedric narrowed his eyes. "Wha' condition?"

"I want the female back."

A low growl ripped from Marc's throat as he swiftly closed the distance between them. Only Cedric's large arm kept him from laying paws on him. "Ye'll no' be getting my Bronaugh back fer yer sick games."

Keegan stood his ground, holding up a hand to Stone, who had also sprung forward at the threat to his pack master. "Not that female. The other one. With the dark spiky hair."

"Bitsy?" Cedric asked. Then he immediately shook his head. "Ye'll no' be getting that one back, either. Bronaugh is part o' my pack now, and Bitsy is her family, which makes *her* part o' my pack. She is under my protection, and never again will she be used for yer games."

But Keegan held up both hands now and attempted to diffuse the situation. They'd misunderstood his intentions. "Everyone calm down. That's not what I want her for."

"Then what *do* ye want her fer?" Cedric asked.

"I want her to help me find the other soul suckers out there. As you yourself said, there's at least fifty of them roaming around. I want her to help me find them." It was an excuse he'd just come up with on the ride up there.

"What fer?"

"For my rodeo, if they're beyond help."

"And if they're no'?"

"Then I will keep them where they can be watched, or hand them over to you." He shrugged. "Whichever you wish."

"Yer a hunter. Ye can find th' dark ones yerself," Marc spit out. "As ye 'ave already proven."

Keegan crossed his arms over his chest. "But that's where you're wrong, my friend. We can find Faeries, sure. However, it's near impossible to figure out which tribe they're from. Even if they tell us, there's no guarantee they're telling the truth."

"As if ye cared," Marc ground out. Fists clenched at his sides, he turned to his Alpha. "Cedric, we cannae agree tae this! Bronough will nae forgive me, or ye, if we try tae take her cousin from her when she only just got her back. She will nae allow it."

Keegan couldn't blame him for being all up in arms about it. He'd seen the rodeo with his own eyes. It wasn't for pussies.

The entire time Marc was shootin' off at the mouth,

Cedric hadn't moved. But those icy blue eyes had held Keegan's, steady and calculating, as though they could see right through to his soul.

When Marc finally paused, he spoke. "We'll ask Bitsy what she wants tae do."

Marc scowled, but Cedric shot him a look.

"'Tis her decision," Cedric told him. "No' ours. We will ask her." With a nod to Keegan, Cedric turned and started walking back to the cars.

Keegan joined him. As they walked, the breath he didn't realize he'd been holding released on a strong exhale.

She would come back.

He would accept nothing less.

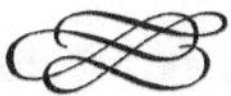

CHAPTER 3

"Bláthnaid Dunn, you cannot do this! I forbid it!"

Bitsy made a face and covered her ears. Her mother only called her that when she was truly upset. The name, pronounced "blaw-nid," meant "little flower." Her father told her once it had been his idea to name her that, because she'd smelled like the wild flowers of Ireland right from the womb. And "Bitsy" had come about because, well, she was a "wee bitsy little thing" as a child.

Bitsy took her mother's hands in hers. "Mom, calm down and listen to me. Please."

"No! No! I will not! You cannot go back there. Have you forgotten what those monsters did to you? To me? To Bronaugh?"

Forget being roped like cattle and dragged around a dirt arena? Or being hit with their electric cattle prods? Not likely. "No, Mom. I haven't forgotten."

"Then why in the world would you want to go back there?"

Good question. "I'm not going back to their 'rodeo', Mom. I'm going to help Asshat find more like us. So I can keep them the fuck away from him and his cowboy games."

"Bitsy! Language," her mother scolded.

But Bitsy could tell it was more out of habit than the fact she was actually paying attention. "Mom, if I go back, *Keegan*"—it took everything she had not to spit the name from her mouth—"will agree to the alliance. If the other packs in the area see this, they'll fall in line. It will save lives. And, what if there are more harmless *an olc* out there like Bronaugh? Or *na maithe*, like us? Innocent Fae that would be caught and made to participate in their games if I'm not there to stop it?"

Her mother pursed her lips and shook her head, her arms crossed over her chest. "I don't trust this. They are shifters. They don't need you. They found *us* without any help."

"And they made us part of their sick sport. Just like they will to any other Fae they find, no matter what tribe they are." Anyone else would take one look at her mother and think the woman was unmovable, but Bitsy could tell she was softening. So, she laid down her best and final argument. The true reason she had agreed to this asinine plan. "What if I can find Dad?"

Her mom dropped her arms to her sides and stared at her. A glimmer of hope in her eyes was there and gone so fast, Bitsy almost missed it. "Your father will find us without you risking your life. We've been together a long time. We have a strong connection. He will find us." Her tone didn't convey the strength of her words.

"Then why hasn't he, Mom?" Bitsy sighed, and took her hands again. "If he was able to find us, he would have been here by now." Her mother looked away, and Bitsy knew she was thinking the same thing Bitsy was—her father wasn't coming because he was hurt, or captured, or worse. "I'm not a little girl. I can take care of myself. And I will find my father. With Keegan along, it will be safer for me than if we tried on our own, or with Cedric. Keegan knows the other packs around him. The risk will be less."

"And what if it's not, Bitsy? What if they lock you behind iron bars again? What will you be able to do then?"

But Bitsy just smiled. "Wolf-man has a thing for me, Mom. He won't be locking me away anywhere, except maybe in his bedroom." Which wouldn't necessarily be a bad thing. *Not* because she had any intention of acting on the attraction between them. That damn wolf had something of hers. And she wanted it back.

Her mom frowned, but then her eyes widened as comprehension smoothed away the lines on her forehead. "Bitsy!"

"Don't act so shocked. It seems to be the nature of the beast around here. They can't seem to resist us."

Her cousin, Bronaugh, gave a snort from her spot on the sofa, where she was pretending not to listen. Her own wolf-man, Marc, had made it very clear that he was completely against the idea of Bitsy going anywhere, but he'd left the three of them alone in the apartment to give them time to speak privately about it.

Bitsy looked back at her, lifting one eyebrow. "You're not helping my case here, Bro."

"Sorry." Bronaugh grinned at her "cousin."

Bitsy rolled her eyes, suppressing a smile. Turning back to her mom, she squeezed her hands. "Mom, I'm doing this. I promise I'll be careful. And I'll be back before you know it. Hopefully, with Dad in tow."

"I just don't know what I would do if I lost you, too." It was the first time her mother had admitted she was frightened the absence of her husband, and Bitsy's father, was permanent.

She took in her mother's beloved features, still handsome even at her age. Her long, dark hair barely had any gray, and her skin was nearly as smooth as a young girl's. However, a wisdom that only came with age shone from her clear, brown eyes. Eyes that were lined with strain from all they'd been through lately. "You won't lose me. I swear it, Mom. Cedric is giving me a phone with a tracking device, and he's sending Lucian and Duncan to a small town right outside of Austin. They'll be near enough, should anything happen."

Her mother, Nancy, wiped a tear from her eye and nodded. "I suppose that's as safe as you can be." Her hand was gentle as she touched Bitsy's cheek. "And you're old enough to make up your own mind. I just wish you wouldn't put yourself in danger while doing it."

Bronaugh came over to them then. "Aunt Nancy, if it makes you feel any better, I've seen the way Keegan looks at her. He may be entirely too full of himself, and a complete asshole—"

"Asshat," Bitsy corrected.

"Asshat," Bronaugh repeated. "But, he won't let anything serious happen to Bits. I honestly believe that."

Bitsy remembered the way he'd looked at her, too. The

Alpha was completely in lust with her, she'd bet her life on it. And if his attraction to her would get her Dad back, then she was prepared to use it to her full advantage.

The fight visibly drained from her mother. "You promise me you will come home. Unharmed!"

Bitsy kissed her on the cheek. "I will. I promise." And then she hugged her tight.

If only she felt as confident as she sounded.

THE NEXT DAY, Bitsy was on her way back to Texas. She rode in the backseat, headphones in her ears the entire trip so she didn't have to listen to Duncan and Lucian constantly bickering. She only had a small backpack with some mix and match clothes and a few necessities. One good thing about keeping her hair so short, it required little to no maintenance. She didn't even need product to make it stick up. It just kind of did it on its own.

As the evergreens faded to brown scrub brush and the majestic mountains flattened out to nothing more than fields of straw-like grass, Bitsy asked herself for the three-hundredth and forty-second time what the fuck she was doing.

But then she'd see her father's laughing brown eyes beyond her own reflection in the window, and her anxiety would settle into a sense of calm purpose. He was out there somewhere, he had to be, and she would do what she had to do to find him.

Except be nice to Keegan. That, she could not do.

But she didn't think it would matter much. Besides, if she was suddenly all sweet as honey after everything he'd put her and her family through, it would bore him. She knew this with a female's instinct. If she wanted him to help her, she needed to keep him interested.

And if things went as she hoped, soon the Fae would no longer have to fear his kind. She was tired of living life in secret, always avoiding everyone and everything. Since the last war between the Fae and the Werewolves, her people had survived by staying in small groups and staying hidden. But that was changing. It had already started, with Brock and Heather, and Marc and Bronaugh.

Not that she planned on being any part of the next interspecies couple. Oh, hell no. She had nothing against dating outside her kind. But she had a whole hell of a lot against the male she was about to be spending most of her time with.

The two wolves in the front seat continued to go at it, oblivious of her presence. Duncan seemed to get his kicks by irritating Lucian until he was spitting mad. At first, Bitsy was worried, afraid Lucian's irritation would get the best of him and he'd shift right there in the driver's seat. But after a few hours, she relaxed.

Because she realized what Duncan was doing. By being such a huge pain in the ass, he was actually helping Lucian learn to keep a grip on himself. The more he pissed him off, the more Lucian had to control his inner wolf. She understood what he was doing, but her headphones only blocked so much, no matter how loud she turned up the music.

Bitsy was real close to reaching up there and knocking their thick skulls together when they passed the exit sign for I-35 to Austin.

Oh, thank the gods.

They arrived in town well after rush hour, and got to her hotel shortly after. Her first stipulation in coming was that there was no way, no how, she was going anywhere near Keegan's ranch, or the fucking barn behind it. The barn that housed the arena for his rodeo. Hell, no. She would stay at a hotel, in the city.

Duncan turned onto 6th street and pulled up to The Driskill hotel shortly thereafter. A thrill ran through Bitsy as she eyed the historic exterior. She'd insisted on staying there. The place was reputed to be haunted, and her inner ghost hunter couldn't resist the opportunity.

Duncan twisted around in the seat. "All right, lass. Here ye go. Ye have yer phone?"

"Yes. And your numbers are programmed into my speed dial."

"Aye. Good. Tha' was my next question." He grinned at her, bright green eyes dancing, so much like Keegan's, and much to her consternation, her stomach did a little flip. "Yer room is paid through th' end o' th' month. If yer here longer, just tell them tae put it on th' card on file."

"Asshat's card?"

Duncan grinned at her. "Tha' would be th' one."

"Okay." Bitsy unplugged her headphones and shoved them into her bag. Her phone she would keep on her person at all times. "Thanks for the ride."

"Ach. Aye. We won't be far. Dinna hesitate tae call fer any reason." He looked past Lucian and out the window. "Seems yer friend is waiting fer ye."

Bitsy followed his line of vision to see Keegan, Alpha of the Texas pack, leaning against the washed-out stone of the building, his buckskin-colored cowboy hat pulled down low over his eyes to protect them from the setting sun. At the sight of him, tall and powerful, butterflies exploded in her gut, a hundred times worse than being on the receiving end of Duncan's flirty smile. The male oozed Alpha. Her eyes traveled from his well-worn cowboy boots, up jeans stretched tight over muscular thighs, to a short-sleeved, unbuttoned plaid shirt, biceps bulging beneath the sleeves. Underneath, he wore a white cotton tank. A silver chain hung around his neck, the pendant nestled at the bottom of his throat.

A shiver ran through Bitsy in spite of the fact that sweat ran down her spine from the Texas heat. Whether it was at the sight of her chain around that tan throat, the male waiting for her, or her body's reaction to him, was left to be determined. "He's not my friend."

No, he'd never be able to just be a friend.

CHAPTER 4

Keegan pushed his hat back on his head. Squinting against the setting sun, he watched as Bitsy got out of the car. She closed her door and leaned over the passenger window, crossing her arms and sticking her head inside—saying something to the males within—and gave him a nice long gander at her rounded bottom, barely covered in cut-off jean shorts. Little as she was, her legs were full and smooth and curvy, and he could almost feel the weight of them wrapped around his neck as he buried his face between her thighs.

A possessive growl rumbled deep in his throat, startling a couple walking past him.

The lady's head snapped around at the sound, lips parted in breathless surprise. Her eyes traveled the length of him and back. She smiled, slowing her steps until she nearly pulled her date to a halt.

Keegan touched the brim of his hat. "Ma'am." Then turned his eyes back to Bitsy's alluring pose.

Her man quickly pulled her away, scowling at Keegan over his shoulder.

Bitsy straightened and waved as the car pulled away, and Keegan tore his eyes away from her ass as she slung her backpack over her shoulder. She didn't turn around right away, and Keegan waited, giving her time to collect herself. Honestly, he was kinda shocked she was there at all. He'd never really expected her to come back of her own free will. Hoped, yes. Expected, no. She had bigger balls than he did, after everything she'd been through the last time she was here.

After everything he'd allowed to happen.

When the seconds turned to minutes, and she still stood on the edge of the sidewalk staring after her ride, Keegan cleared his throat.

With a long-suffering sigh he heard even from behind her, Bitsy turned around. Her chin lifted high, and she somehow managed to look down her nose at him from her diminutive height. She'd filled out a bit since he'd last seen her. She was even cuter than he remembered.

"Hey, Bitsy."

Her eyes dropped to the chain around his neck. "I want my necklace back."

He tried for a smile. "Not one to beat around the bush, are ya?"

The look of disgust on her face gave away her thoughts before she spoke them. "No. I'm not. You've given me no reason to be tactful."

"You're welcome to come get it." His stomach tightened with excitement at the thought of her touching him.

She seemed to consider it, but then she crossed her

arms and held her ground. "Why are you doing this? We both know you and your pack don't need any help finding Fae." Her lips curled into a sneer. "Either tribe."

She was referring to the fact that she and her mother were *na maithe*, the "good" kind of Faeries, if any Faeries were truly good, the kind that didn't pose any danger to anyone. Keegan hadn't realized what tribe Bitsy and her mom were from when they'd first been brought to the ranch, and by the time he had, releasing them would've caused more problems than he'd wanted to deal with.

Keegan took off his hat, running a hand through his freshly cut hair. It was still damn hot, even this late in the year. "Look, I didn't know you and your momma weren't Dark Fae. Lord knows, there's no easy way to tell y'all apart."

Bitsy lifted one eyebrow. Her warm brown eyes somehow frosty as the inside of a deep freeze. "Maybe the fact that we weren't smashing our own heads bloody against the bars every time you came near us should've clued you in."

His face heated, but he swallowed down the feeling of shame. He knew what she thought of him, but she had no idea what it took to lead a pack of werewolves, or how far he would go to keep them from tearing apart the town they lived in. Without anything else to occupy them, they needed some way to blow off steam. His rodeo provided that. Good, old school Texas fun. Bitsy and her mom had just been in the wrong place at the wrong time.

However, it was a mistake he wouldn't let happen again. "You have no intention of helping me find more Fae for my rodeo." He didn't try to close the distance between them, knowing in spite of the brave front she was putting on, she was as skittish as a rabbit. And he couldn't say he blamed her.

"Nope."

Keegan licked his lower lip, his mouth suddenly dry. "Yet, you came anyway." He set his hat back on his head. "I know it's hard for you see, but the rodeo was a good thing—"

She turned her face away, but not before he saw the look of disgust.

He pressed on. "I needed to keep it going because if I didn't, my wolves wouldn't have an outlet for the aggression that builds up inside—especially the unmated ones. And that means they'll find some other way to let loose, whether it be fighting amongst themselves, or coming into the city here to blow off steam. Either option is bad news for the pack."

"You're unmated. I never saw you anything *but* controlled. Why can't they do the same?"

"It's not always as easy as all that, ittybit."

She narrowed her eyes at the nickname that had slipped out from nowhere, but didn't let it distract her from her questions. "Why not?"

He eased a bit closer to her, close enough to catch her scent in the still dry air. She smelled like moonflowers and sun-warmed skin. She smelled like home.

"Why not, Ass—Keegan?" she repeated. "If you can't control your pack, maybe you don't need to be their Alpha."

Her words struck hard in places he didn't want to examine too closely. He took another step closer, until he was towering over her. "I'm their Alpha because I fought my way into this position. And I don't need some uppity Fae chick telling me how to control my wolves."

A normal female would be intimidated by a large male such as him, but not this one. In spite of her small stature, she stared up at him with a blatant challenge in her eyes. "Maybe I wouldn't need to if you had what it took to be a good leader."

They glared at each other, caught at an impasse. Goddamn, but she made him hard. Still, Keegan was the one who backed off. She was only trying to goad him. She didn't need to know how much her words struck home. Or how much he enjoyed her smart mouth. It would only add fuel to her fire. He offered her a tight smile. "My leadership skills, or lack thereof, aren't up for discussion. What *is* on the table is why you came back."

She turned her head away, watching a group of humans come toward them. "There's something I want from you. Other than my necklace back."

His pulse raced, but he gave her a nod. "Name it."

"I want you to help me find my father. He was separated from mom and me when your gang of mutts cornered and captured us. I want you to help me find him, and I want him to go home to my mother."

The fact that she hadn't included herself in that scenario didn't escape him. "So, I help you find dear old dad, and you'll grace me with your presence. That's the deal?"

After a moment's pause, she nodded. "Yes."

"What if I don't want to give this back?" He looped the

chain he was wearing over his thumb, holding it out for her to see.

Her eyes dropped to the tree pendant. Several seconds ticked by. "Keep it," she gritted out through clenched teeth.

She wasn't fooling him. The chain meant more to her than she was letting on. It's why he took it from her. It was something that would link them together.

"You got it, ittybit." He dropped the necklace and stuck out his hand, and after a long moment, she took it. Her hand was ice cold, in spite of the heat, and he covered it with both of his own. He tightened his grip on hers and caught her eyes. "No harm will come to you here, you have my word."

She nodded, and pulled her hand out from between his. He clenched his fists, unconsciously seeking the warmth of her skin against his. "One last thing," he told her.

"What's that?"

"While you're here, you need to pretend to like me. At least when we're around others."

A very unladylike snort made him smile. "Why the hell would I do that?"

"So I can keep you alive. If the others think you're with me, they won't dare do anything to hurt you. You can hate me all you want when we're alone, shoot daggers at me with your eyes, cuss at me...whatever. But around others, I'm your moon and stars and you'll be mine."

"Even around your own pack?"

"Especially around my own pack."

"Which takes me back to my former argument."

He had to admire her tenacity. "Just do as I tell you, Bitsy. Or I can't be held responsible for what happens to you."

Her eyes flew to his, and he realized he'd practically growled the words at her. He was getting too caught up in the nearness of her, and he took a step back. "I don't want anything to happen to you, is all. I promised Cedric I would keep you safe if you agreed to come back. And I intend to keep that promise."

"Did I really have a choice?"

"I'll always give you a choice, ittybit."

"You wouldn't have agreed to the alliance if I hadn't come."

"Nope. But you still had the choice."

She gazed down the street in the direction her ride had gone, a wistful expression on her face, then turned back to him. "Well then, I might as well get checked in." With purpose to her steps, she walked past him and he followed.

"Are you sure you won't come stay at the ranch? In the house, this time," he added when she shot him a look so full of venom, he was surprised his blood hadn't turned to acid in his veins.

"I'm fucking positive," she said. "I'm staying here."

"Do you kiss your momma with that mouth?"

"Every fucking day."

A young human male opened the door to the hotel for her. He tipped his hat as she passed, and she gave him a smile that made his heart stutter.

Keegan knew this for a fact, because he heard it. It echoed the noise going on in his own chest. He cleared his throat, maybe bowed up a bit, for the young male jumped.

"So sorry, sir." Moving out of the way, he held the door for Keegan.

He touched the brim of his hat politely even as he bared his teeth. "Keep your eyes in your head, kid. She's off limits."

The male's eyes widened to such a size it was almost comical as he took in the full impression of the Alpha wolf standing before him. "Y-Yes, sir." Dropping his eyes, he stepped back and waited for Keegan to pass.

"Have a good day now, kid, ya hear?" He searched the lobby for Bitsy, impressed as ever by the old hotel—grand columns throughout and stained glass on the ceiling to let in the light. He found her over by the check-in desk. As he approached, he heard the desk clerk confirming the room Keegan had booked for her.

"All right, miss. So, we have you booked in one of our Petite Queen rooms. I think you'll enjoy it. These rooms are small, as they used to be the servant rooms, but they've been remodeled and upgraded. So though cozy, they still provide every comfort."

Keegan moseyed up to the desk and leaned his back against it, resting his elbows on the counter as he kept an eye on the comings and goings of the humans.

"Yeah, about that. Do you have any other rooms available? Something larger, maybe?" Bitsy's voice practically dripped honey.

What was the little hellcat up to, now?

The clerk set the room key he'd been holding down on the desk and consulted his computer screen. "It seems we have a Landmark Suite available for an indefinite amount of time, but they are triple the cost of the Petite Queens."

"How much?" Bitsy asked.

"Landmark Suites run $342 per overnight stay, not including tax and fees."

Bitsy looked over at Keegan and gave him a naughty grin. "I'll take it."

Keegan ran his eyes over her pixie face, his heart pounding in his chest at the promises in that smile. He barely heard the rest of the conversation.

"Shall I put it on the card on file?" The clerk glanced at Keegan politely.

It took him a moment to realize he was waiting for a response. "No."

"Yes," Bitsy said at the same time.

Keegan pushed off the counter. "Excuse us a minute, please." Grabbing Bitsy by the wrist, he tried to ignore how tiny it felt in his hand as he pulled her out of hearing range. "What the hell are you doing?"

"Securing my room," she told him matter-of-factly as she yanked her arm out of his grasp.

"Miss?" The clerk was watching them, his forehead wrinkled in concern. "Is everything all right?" He eyed Keegan nervously.

"Everything's fine," she told him with a smile. "Would you go ahead and book that room and get me my room key, please?"

With another nervous look between them, the clerk nodded. "Of course. One or two?"

"Two," Keegan told him. It would save him from paying for damages.

"One." She narrowed her eyes at Keegan. "One," she stated firmly.

They faced off, feet planted, eyes staring daggers at each other, until Keegan gave in. Tearing his eyes from the fierce female in front of him before he busted out the zipper on his pants, he gave the clerk a nod. "Fine. One."

With a sigh of relief, the male placed one key on the desk. "Room 301."

Bitsy walked over and grabbed it up. "Thanks." She leaned in against the counter. "So, are there really ghosts here?"

The clerk gave her a secret smile. "That's the rumor. Be sure to let me know if you see any."

"I will," she told him in all seriousness. Ignoring Keegan completely, she picked up her backpack and headed to the wide staircase that would take her to her room.

He shuffled along behind her, his blood still racing from their contest of wills. As they made their way to her room, he squinted into the corners, every hair on his body standing on end.

She just had to pick the most notoriously haunted hotel in Austin.

CHAPTER 5

Bitsy slammed the door in Keegan's face with a sense of satisfaction. Just for good measure, she locked the deadbolt and slid the chain. It wouldn't keep him out if he truly wanted to get in, but it certainly got her message across.

She needed a little time to herself before setting out on a Faerie hunt with him. Time to figure out what the hell she'd been thinking by agreeing to come back here, after she'd sworn to herself she would never set foot in Texas again, and certainly not anywhere near the local Alpha who didn't have the balls to stop something he knew was wrong.

Dropping her pack on the marble floor, she left it there and checked out the room—the Yellow Rose Landmark.

"*Holy* shit."

The room was like a small apartment. She wandered into the living space, admiring the Persian rug that matched the rich earth tones of the furniture for a minute before checking out the rest of the room. To her left was a small table with two chairs, and along the wall was a desk for the businessy types. To her right must be the bed and bath area. Floor to ceiling windows allowed plenty of light.

The room even had crown molding, for gods' sake.

She found the bedroom, admired the tapestry poster bed and the armoire, then peeked into the bathroom.

More marble. Black this time. "Wow." She planned on making use of that tub before the night was out.

Staying in a place like this would almost make it all worth it, if she was a materialistic kind of female. But, unfortunately for her conscience, she wasn't.

She did enjoy a good soak in the tub, though.

Bitsy fell on the bed and stared up at the fancy ceiling, wondering how long it would take to find her father. She hated the south in general, and Texas in particular. It was too fucking hot. Or too fucking cold. Depending on the time of year. She much preferred the temperate climates of the cool, wet north. East or West, rain or snow, she didn't care. She didn't care what country, either, though she did appreciate the many different cultures of Europe over the US.

Not to mention, there were no Faerie rodeos in Europe. In the old country, the Fae were treated with the fear and respect they deserved.

Her head pounded so hard her vision blurred as she remembered everything her family had gone through at the paws of these meat-headed mutts. Sitting up, she took deep breaths until she felt her pulse return to normal. If it hadn't been for the iron cages they'd been kept in, weakening her to the point of a human, she would've killed every single one of those sons of bitches.

Well, maybe not Keegan. She might have kept him alive for a while so she could enjoy watching him beg her forgiveness.

She lay back down and clenched her jaw. Allowing him to live was more than he deserved. He'd stood there and *watched*, uncaring, while she and her mother were dragged around the arena with chains and ropes. Like animals. While they were injured, laughed at…humiliated.

And yet, she'd felt a thrill go through her every time his green eyes met hers. She'd felt it again the moment she'd seen him leaning up against the side of the hotel, hat low over his brow, thumbs hooked in his belt loops, his overwhelming maleness making her heart stutter in her chest. She'd had to take a minute to get her traitorous body under control, talking to Duncan and Lucian, so he wouldn't see how much he affected her.

As Bitsy lay there, scowling up at the crown molding, the fine hair on her arms suddenly stood straight up. She sat up and looked around the room, all thoughts of Keegan forgotten for the moment. "Hello?" No one answered her, but she couldn't shake the feeling that she wasn't the only one in the room.

Her heart pounded with a different kind of excitement. Call her strange, but there was nothing Bitsy loved more than chatting with the dead. It fascinated her to learn about their lives, and how those lives had ended. "Hello? Is someone there? It's okay. You can show yourself." She held her breath and waited, but no one appeared.

The feeling slowly dissipated, and she found herself alone once more.

Bitsy released her breath with a huff of disappointment, got up to retrieve her pack from the entryway, and went back to cursing Keegan McRae the entire way. It was his fault her father had become separated from them, and somehow, she knew it was his fault she had to come back down here to get him.

But if he thought she could be played with, that male had a hell of a surprise coming his way. She was going to get her father home to her mother if it was the last thing she did. And then she was leaving.

An hour later, Bitsy was just getting out of the bathtub when there was a knock on her door. Assuming it was the room service she'd ordered, she wrapped the large white towel around her and went to answer the door.

But to her surprise, it wasn't a smiling member of the hotel staff with a large tray of food for her, but a scowling Alpha wolf who took up the entire doorway.

"Is this how you always answer the door?"

Bitsy wondered what he had up his ass this time. "Opening the door in question is the normal procedure when someone knocks."

"And you couldn't find any clothes to wear before you opened it?"

She smiled like a Cheshire cat. "I thought you were someone else."

He snarled at that. Literally snarled. Without waiting for an invitation, he pushed his way past her, shutting the door behind him.

Before Bitsy knew what was happening, his hat was on

the floor and he had her up against the wall, palms flat beside her head. She squeaked in surprise, her hands going to his heavy shoulders like they belonged there, his hard body the only thing holding up her towel. "What the hell are you doing?"

"Fight me." His deep voice shook, and his eyes were feverish as they darted over her bare skin. "*Fight* me, Bitsy," he gritted out.

His scent surrounded her—clean male and wilderness — as he trembled against her. The blood rushed through her veins at the sense of suppressed power within him. She opened her mouth to shoot him down with a smartass comment, but it fell silent from her lips. Her chest tightened until she almost couldn't breathe as the truth rose within her. "I don't want to fight you," she told him softly.

Bitsy had no time to take it back before his mouth came down hard on hers. She shoved at his shoulders half-heartedly, but he just growled deep in his throat and took both wrists in one hand, pinning them above her head. He took what he wanted with lips that were firm but soft and fitted perfectly to hers.

Momentarily stunned by the warmth flooding her body until she half expected to burst into flames, Bitsy froze. But not for long.

Sucking his bottom lip into her mouth, she bit down as hard as she could. With a grunt, Keegan pulled away, but not far. His tongue touched the blood she'd drawn, his green eyes burning bright.

"I hate you," she spit at him. And she did. In that moment, she did hate him, for showing her it didn't matter.

His lips curved into a sad semblance of a smile. "I know."

They stared at each other, nothing but the sound of their heavy breaths between them. Bitsy could feel his sex, swollen and hot, pressed against her belly. And much as she tried to fight it, her body responded, blood rushing to the surface, heating and sensitizing her skin.

Keegan moved slightly, and the towel rubbed her sensitive nipples. A moan escaped her before she could stop it, and a part of her wished the damn thing would just fall already. The other part of her wished her hands were free so she could strangle him with it. "Let me go."

His eyes glowed from beneath his heavy brows. "I can't."

His voice was like gravel, and Bitsy knew he was fighting his nature as much as she was. She opened her mouth. Whether it was to curse him out or beg him to kiss her again, she didn't know.

Keegan lowered his head until his mouth was only an inch from hers. But he went no farther.

How could he tease her like this? A sound escaped her, something between need and denial, and finally, *finally*, he took the choice out of her hands, and again captured her lips with his. She tasted the copper tang of his blood, and the sweet heat of his need.

It matched her own.

The kiss went on forever, and yet ended all too soon. Keegan released her wrists, and her hands fell to his shoulders again as he dropped little kisses on her lips, her nose, her throat.

Bitsy dug her fingers into his dark hair, curling her

fingers until she knew it had to hurt him, but he didn't say a word. She pulled his head up until she could look him in the eye. "I hate you." They seemed to be the only words she was capable of speaking.

He smiled that sad smile, little lines crinkling around his eyes from the sun. "I know, ittybit."

He stepped away, and she grabbed for her towel before it could fall.

His eyes fell to the tops of her breasts. "I'll be here to get you first thing in the morning," he told her. Picking up his hat, he gave her one more hot glance and yanked open the door.

A young woman stood there with her arm raised to knock. Her eyes dropped to the bulge in his pants, and her face turned red before they quickly rose back up to his face. "Room service," she croaked.

"That's for me." Bitsy pushed the overbearing asshat out of the way and pointed at the table. "Just put it over there, please. And add a big tip for yourself to the card on file."

The woman kept her head down as she pushed the cart into the room with Bitsy's dinner. Okay, it was probably enough to feed her for a week. But, hey, she was hungry, and she wasn't paying for it.

Asshat was.

"Be ready in the morning," was all he said, and stormed out of the room with barely a glance at the fortune in food on the table.

Staring after him, Bitsy found she'd lost her appetite.

CHAPTER 6

Keegan walked down Austin's infamous 6th street beside the college kids and tourists, his mind spinning and his dick hurting something fierce. He hadn't planned on going back to Bitsy's room. And he certainly hadn't planned on kissing her once he got there. But she'd opened the door in nothing but that fluffy, white towel, her dark hair sticking out all over her head, her brown eyes spewing surprise instead of hatred, and he'd lost every coherent thought in his head.

He scrubbed his face with hands and readjusted his hat. Bringing her back down here may not have been the best idea he'd ever had. She hated his guts, and he couldn't honestly say he blamed her.

But, dammit, he'd missed the little spitfire.

When he'd first seen her and her mom, huddled together in the iron cell where his trappers had thrown them shortly after they'd been captured, Keegan had known they weren't soul suckers. Not from any visible trait they had, but because of the way they were looking at the two crazy ones in the cell next to them. Those two *were* soul suckers—from the *an olc* Fae tribe—gone to the dark side. There was no sadness in either of the female's eyes for the loss of a couple of their own, only fear. And on Bitsy's part, disgust.

She'd caught his notice right off—a fiery little Faerie with spiky hair, curvy chest and hips, and dark, expressive eyes lit by a promise for vengeance. There was no fear in those eyes. Not for the soul suckers. Not for him. Not for his pack.

As he'd stood there staring at her, she'd whispered something to the other female in the cell with her, stood up without taking her eyes from his, walked over to the bars, and flipped him off. She'd stared right at him the entire time, hatred twisting her perfect lips into a sneer.

And his dick had grown hard as a rock.

Keegan grinned just thinking about it.

At the time, he'd chuckled, ordered the others to check the locks, and then he'd spun on the heel of his snakeskin boot and left the room. But he couldn't stop thinking about the little hellion they'd managed to wrangle into his barn.

He'd wondered if he'd be able to tame her. And the more he'd wondered, the more it became a challenge he couldn't resist. Going against his gut, he'd allowed her to be a part of the rodeo, but he *had* limited her to only certain events. He'd done the same for the other female, so as not to be seen showing favoritism, and he'd quieted the protests by letting his wolves do whatever the hell they wanted to the soul suckers.

But his little hellion would not break. As a matter of fact, the more they did to her, the more defiant she became, and the more she gained his respect.

And the worse he began to feel for doing what he was doing to her.

He'd gone in to see her once when the other female was in the arena. She was pacing her cell, worry for the other one plain on her elfin face, as she ignored the two crazy ones throwing themselves into the bars of the next cell. When she realized he was standing there, watching her, she stopped. Her eyes met his, but she didn't say anything. She didn't need to. He could read everything she was thinking in her animated face.

And she was thinking a lot of things, all aimed at him. And none of it was good. As a matter of fact, he would wager that most, if not all, of it concerned the various ways she wanted to kill him. In the most painful way possible.

Keegan had walked closer, seeking to reassure her. "I promise your friend will come back relatively unharmed."

"She's my mother, Asshat. And if she doesn't, you'll wish to the gods you never laid eyes on me."

He fell a little bit in love with her that day.

That was the last time he went to go see her alone, because he didn't trust himself not to lock himself in that cell with her, and not leave until he somehow managed to convince her to let him kiss her. The odds of that happening weren't in his favor, he had to admit. And he couldn't say he blamed her. Letting her go, however, had never crossed his mind. Because he knew if he did, he would never see her again.

The next time he saw her, he was wearing her chain. His second in command had confiscated it when she'd been searched before she was thrown into the cell. And Keegan made sure she'd noticed. If for no other reason than to make sure she wouldn't forget him. It was fucked up. He knew it. The whole thing was fucked up.

But he couldn't seem to stop himself.

Then Marc showed up from the Seattle pack with his crazy alliance talk, and Keegan had been too busy to visit her again. To add to the excitement, another Fae female had been caught right outside their barn. It ended up she *was* a Dark Fae, but she was also Marc's mate. And then all hell had broken loose. Next thing he new, his little spitfire was leaving the same way she had come in.

Flipping off a bunch of werewolves.

Keegan had let her go, knowing she wasn't going far, and also knowing if the Seattle pack wanted their alliance so bad, he now had something to bargain with to get her back. And it had worked.

Her father was a glitch in his plan he hadn't expected, but he could deal with it. And it had brought her back to him. He'd find her old man, and when he did, maybe she wouldn't hate him quite so much.

And maybe, someday, she'd do something he would never be able to.

Forgive him.

Keegan sighed. He should keep his paws off her. At least until she had a chance to see he wasn't the unfeeling bastard she believed him to be.

Finding a little corner bar that wasn't too crowded, Keegan pulled up a stool and settled in for the night. He wouldn't be going back out to the ranch. Stone could manage everything there while he was gone. Nope, he was staying close to his female. If she'd stayed at any other hotel in the city, he would've gotten a room there, too.

But no, she had to stay at The Driskill.

That damn hotel was haunted. Not rumored to be. It *was.* The energy in the place made Keegan's fur stand on end as soon as he entered the building, and there was no way in hell he was spending an entire night there in a room all by himself. Call him a chickenshit, but any other werewolf would understand. That kind of shit creeped them the hell out. Witches, ghosts, or any of that magic heebie-jeebie stuff. It wasn't natural. When people died, they should be dead and gone, not hanging around scaring the boots off those who had the gall to still be alive.

Keegan's cell phone vibrated, and he pulled it out of his pocket and looked at the screen. It was a text from Merrick, the Alpha of the Colorado pack. He wasn't a friend, but he wasn't an enemy, either. And he and his pack traveled down to Austin at least once a month to take part in the rodeo. Keegan had made some calls before he'd gone back to Bitsy's room, putting out some feelers, to see what he could find out about her father.

We found something that may interest you.

Keegan smiled.

Lay it on me.

The bartender came over and he ordered a whiskey. Straight. It was going to be a long night, but hopefully

Merrick had some info he could take to Bitsy in the morning.

THE NEXT MORNING, after running back to the ranch to shower and pack a bag, Keegan knocked on Bitsy's door at exactly 7 am. "Rise and shine, ittybit. It's time to get some grub and get going."

"Fuck off."

The words were far away and muffled, even to his superior hearing.

He knocked again, louder this time.

"I said, FUCK off."

Loud and clear this time.

He grinned. Weren't the Fae supposed to be all in tune with nature and shit, and therefore, morning people by default? "So, I guess you don't want to go follow this possible lead I have on your old man?" He leaned back against the wall and crossed his arms over his chest. Silently, he counted.

One...

Two...

Three...

The locks were thrown amongst some more cursing, and the door to Bitsy's room was flung open. She popped her head out, looking down the hall before finally spotting him on the other side. "What did you say?"

Keegan pushed away from the wall and ran his eyes over her. She was ridiculously adorable in an oversized T-shirt with a rainbow-colored unicorn on the front. Her hair was flat against her head on one side and stuck straight out on the other.

And, she was only wearing one purple sock.

He cocked an eyebrow, looking pointedly at her foot, and waited for an explanation, one that would make any kind of sense in her world. He wasn't disappointed.

"What? My foot gets cold."

"Only the right one?"

"Yes. Only the right one." She rolled her eyes. "What were you saying about my father?"

"Let me in and I'll tell you."

To his surprise, she immediately stepped back and held the door open for him. Keegan stepped over the threshold, took his hat off and set it on the desk, then ran a hand through his hair. He took a look around, something he'd been too distracted to do the night before, and whistled, loud and long. "Whooee. This is a damn fine room I'm paying for."

"It is. But it's the least you can do after you allowed your wolves to electrocute my happy ass every other day. Not to mention the lack of a toilet, or any privacy at all, for that matter. And let's not even get into our neighbors —the two soul suckers in the next cell, constantly eye fucking my perfectly functioning brain. When they weren't slamming their heads into the bars and spitting at us." She raised one eyebrow. "Shall I go on?"

Keegan's cheerful mood disintegrated into dust. He turned to face her with his heart in his throat. "I'm sorry for doing that to you and your family." And he meant it. He may be an "asshat," but he was truly sorry for what he'd allowed. If there had been any way to extricate her and her mom from the situation without causing an uprising, he would've done it. As it was, he'd done what he could to make sure they hadn't been seriously hurt. At least until Jace, his second, had taken it upon himself to decide what events they'd be participating in.

Keegan kinda wished he'd had the opportunity to knock some sense into the shithead before Marc had killed him.

She stared at him a moment, her gaze steady but undecipherable. "I don't forgive you." Then she spun around and headed to what he assumed was the bedroom, slamming the door behind her. A minute later, he heard the shower come on.

The room service menu was open on the small table, so Keegan heaved a sigh and picked it up. He had planned on stopping for something quick, but perhaps he could woo her with food. Come to think of it, he liked the idea of having a little more privacy while they ate. Unsure what she liked or didn't like, he picked up the phone and ordered a little bit of everything, along with some coffee and orange juice. At the last minute, he added coconut water. Just in case.

He wasn't worried about the money. He had plenty of that. Any supernatural creature worth their salt had figured out how to invest by now, and how to live off those investments. Some of them even had their own businesses, both large and small, as did Keegan and his pack with the rodeo, for a little something extra. Multiple streams of income, that was the way to do it.

So, no. The money wasn't an issue. And if it would make his little Fae feel better thinking she was getting one up on him, he was more than happy to let her make a big ole dent in his wallet. It was the very least he could do.

Maybe, someday, she'd even accept his apology.

But until that day, he had his work cut out for him. At least she hadn't tried to take a heavy object to his head… yet. As a matter of fact, she'd been downright congenial, all things considered.

The heaviness weighing on his soul lifted just a bit. Perhaps she didn't hate him quite as much as she claimed.

By the time Bitsy came out, dressed in jean short overalls, an old-fashioned pink lacy top, and modern-style combat boots with mismatched socks peeking out the top, he had their breakfast buffet spread out across the desk and table.

At her look of surprise, he shrugged. "I wasn't sure what you liked."

She gave him a wary look as she eyeballed the food. Her little pink tongue licked her lips, but she made no move toward it.

"It's safe to eat." He had a hard time keeping the amusement out of his voice. "I ordered room service."

Giving him a little side eye, she nonetheless grabbed her plate and helped herself to pancakes and potatoes, adding a blueberry muffin slathered with butter to top it all off.

A carb girl. He'd have to remember that.

Once they both had their plates and cups filled and sat down to eat, Keegan told her what Stone had texted to him at the bar the night before. "My sources tell me there's the distinct possibility there's a group of Fae about a day's ride from here, including an older male."

She stopped chewing. "How reliable are your sources?"

"Reliable enough." The hope on her face was almost too much for him to take. "Don't look at me like that, ittybit. It might not be him, but I think it's worth checking out."

"Where are they?"

"Just across the border of Oklahoma. In Colorado."

Bitsy shoved a forkful of pancakes into her mouth, nodding as she chewed. She swallowed and took a drink of coconut water. "That makes perfect sense."

"Why is that?"

"It's where your wolves found us."

Keegan stopped with his fork halfway to his mouth and narrowed his eyes. "That can't be right."

"Well, it is."

He put down the silverware and sat back in his chair. "No. That ain't right, ittybit. My wolves wouldn't cross the border without my permission."

"Why not?"

"Because that would be trespassing onto another pack's territory. And if they did that without my permission, it could cause a whole shit ton of trouble to come down on my head."

She took a bite of her muffin, chewing thoughtfully. "Guess it's a good thing Jace is dead then, huh? Because he obviously didn't give a rat's ass about your head, or any other part of you."

Son of a bitch.

"I'm finished." Bitsy took a gulp of her coffee, another of orange juice, and chugged down her coconut water.

She got up, paused, and shoved another forkful of potatoes in her mouth. "Okay, let's go."

Keegan finished his coffee and stood. "You're gonna need warmer clothes."

She gave him a wide-eyed look. "Then it looks like we're going shopping."

Bitsy threw her new, oversized backpack behind the passenger seat in Keegan's truck. It was stuffed full with all of the lightweight, cold weather clothes he'd just bought for her, more than she needed for one night of camping. But when she'd piled it all on the counter by the register, he'd pulled out his credit card and paid the ridiculous bill without so much as a lift of his eyebrow.

However, he'd drawn the line at buying her her own tent. And this was after she'd tried every argument she could think of to get him to agree to a hotel room. But apparently, the wolves of the Colorado wolf pack were outdoorsy types. Where they were going, there were no civil accommodations near enough to suit Keegan.

Personally, she thought he just wanted to get her alone in the wilderness.

She wasn't quite sure how she felt about that. Her nether regions were super excited about the prospect, but her heart wasn't nearly as eager.

"So, where exactly are we headed?" she asked once they'd gotten on the highway. Glancing over at the male beside her, she ran her eyes over his powerful body, easily perceived because he was still wearing nothing but jeans and a short-sleeved plaid shirt unbuttoned over a white T-shirt. But when he glanced her way, she quickly averted her eyes and gazed out the windshield.

His presence filled the large cab, and not just his impressive physical form. The entire truck smelled like him—a seductive combination of his aftershave, the natural musk of the outdoors, and something that was purely male.

All extremely irresistible to a Faerie girl like her. If he wasn't such a cold-hearted, sadistic bastard, and if her father's well being wasn't on her mind, this partnership might have had the potential to turn into a hell of a good time. But after what he and his pack of mongrels had done to her and her family, it was nothing but a necessary evil to spend this much time with him. The fact that she was physically attracted to him was her own personal cross to bear.

"We're heading to the mountains just over the border. I've contacted Merrick, and they're expecting us. We'll camp for the night and see what we can find out about the group of Fae first thing tomorrow."

"Why not tonight?"

"Because it's a wolf thing. And because I'll be tired."

This wasn't acceptable to Bitsy. She wanted to find her father, or not, and get the hell back to her hotel. And put some distance between her and the sex god beside her. She adjusted her position, angling her body away from him and settling in for the ride. "You can sleep. I can go find the group myself."

"Hell, no, you won't."

She frowned at his tone and twisted around to look at him. "Why the *hell* not?" She emphasized the curse word, knowing it got under his skin to hear her talk like that.

His hands tightened on the wheel until his knuckles turned white. "Do you know what could happen to you if any of Merrick's pack found you out in those woods? All alone?"

"I have a pretty good idea." Her voice dripped with sarcasm.

Keegan was silent for a good long while after that, and Bitsy turned back to stare out the window. She thought she'd shut him up for a while, but then his voice came from behind her, fast and harsh, like the words were being torn from his throat.

"I did what I could to keep you and your mom from being seriously hurt."

She barked out a laugh, twisting around to face him fully. "Is that so? Well, then, I'd hate to know what would've fucking happened if you hadn't been there to protect us." Her entire body shook with rage. How dare he try to defend what he did?

"I made rules, ittybit. They weren't supposed to put you in the ring with the soul suckers. They weren't supposed to do half the things they did. That was all Jace. But if I'd made a big fuss about it, it would've brought even more attention to you. And not the good kind. There was nothing else I could've done at that point."

"You could've let us go," she spit at him.

He glanced over at her, his green eyes dark with emotion. "I *did* let you go."

He did. And he never came after them as he'd threatened. She turned away from the intensity of his stare. "Not soon enough."

"I told you. I had to keep you there to keep the peace. I had no fucking choice."

"You always have a choice." She threw his own words back at him.

The muscles in his jaw clenched and released. Without another word, his foot punched down on the gas.

Bitsy proceeded to ignore him. Or at least she tried to.

The rest of the ride was spent in blessed silence, except to tell him to get off the highway when she needed a rest stop. It was well past dark when they pulled off the back road they'd been traveling on for the last hour and a half and onto a hidden dirt road. They followed the base of a mountain for a while, before veering off and starting to climb. Keegan threw the truck into 4-wheel drive as they wound in and out of the trees at a steady pace and climbed the mountain.

Bitsy's ears were starting to pop when he finally pulled over and shut off the truck. Immediately, the winter cold began to seep into the cab of the truck. Still in her shorts, she couldn't stop herself from shivering.

Pulling her jacket from the back seat, Keegan handed it to Bitsy. "Stay here. Lock the doors. I'll be right back."

"I want to come with you." Not because she desired his company, but because she didn't want to be left sitting alone in the dark.

He shook his head. "Not this time, ittybit. I need to go

talk to Merrick. It's safer for you here. Then I'll come back and get you."

She didn't like it, but she didn't have a death wish, either. "Fine."

"I'll be back soon." He opened the door and hopped out, shutting it behind him.

She felt the truck rock and turned around to watch him climb into the bed.

Keegan lifted his nose and sniffed the air. He looked around, his hands on the front of his shirt. It took her a minute to realize he was removing it.

By the light of the moon, she could see the powerful muscles of his shoulders—both covered in black ink—as he tossed it into the truck bed. His white tank followed, and Bitsy was suddenly very glad she couldn't see anything else as he hopped down and bent over, out of sight.

She'd seen him in all his glory once before, at the last rodeo, right before her cousin and her mate had saved them all. It wasn't a memory she'd be forgetting anytime soon.

His boots landed in the truck bed with a thud, one by one. In the rearview mirror, she saw his socks and jeans fly over the side.

It was suddenly damn hot, despite the cold air outside. Sounds came to her ears—snapping bones accompanied by the wet sucking of tearing skin and muscle. Keegan's grunt was the only indication of the pain it caused him to shift.

Bitsy didn't want to watch, but she couldn't seem to get her body to obey what her mind was telling it. As a matter of fact, it did the exact opposite, scooting over to the driver's seat so she could see him out the window. She'd seen werewolves turn before, but it never ceased to fascinate her.

Half covered in fur, he was bent over at a strange angle. Head down, his back heaved with his deep breaths. As she watched, his jaw elongated, stretching into the snout of his wolf. Long, sharp teeth appeared in the open mouth. He fell onto all fours, his body contorting and reforming in ways that shouldn't be possible, until his human form was gone.

He shook his large body like a dog, huffing in the cold air. Suddenly, the large head swung around and looked right at her, as though reminding her of her promise to stay in the truck, before he trotted off into the wilderness and left her alone.

It all happened in less than a minute.

Bitsy scooted back to her seat, her heart pounding and her breathing ragged. She was glad he was gone and wasn't there to witness her reaction. All alone, she stopped trying to deny there was something unspoken between them. Something earthy and raw and urgent. She hated him. Hated everything about him. From his southern drawl to his wannabe cowboy attire and powerful aura of the Alpha that surrounded him. She wanted to tear him down. Wanted him raw and exposed. Wanted him to feel even a fraction of the helplessness she had felt in his rodeo. But the truth was, he was an Alpha, born and bred. He was hard, and dangerous at his core, and his wolf called to the wildness in her soul.

She hated him, and she hated the fact that her body didn't hate him at all.

Bitsy drew in a deep breath, but the air in the truck—heavy with the scent of him—was too thick and hard to breathe. She felt light-headed as she tried to roll down the window. Her lungs struggled to suck in air, but he'd taken the keys, so she unlocked the door and propped it open with her foot. Breathing deep of the cold, crisp air, she closed her eyes and concentrated on her father.

Her eyes snapped open a few seconds later. Her dad was here. She could feel him. And he wasn't very far.

Excitement made her forget her promise and throw caution to the wind. Bitsy jumped down out of the truck, grabbing her jacket only as an afterthought. She turned in a circle, getting her bearings, and started off in the opposite direction Keegan had gone.

If she could find her father on her own, tonight, she could be done with this farce.

Bitsy followed her instincts, stopping every now and again to refocus her radar, so to speak. Her bare legs were freezing. But she paid little attention to the cold. She was getting close. She could feel it in her gut.

Something rustled in the underbrush to her right and Bitsy froze. But it was only a fat, brown rabbit. When it saw her there, it bounded away, white tail flashing in danger.

Bitsy watched it flee, then cautiously looked around. She had startled it, yes, but something else caused it to flee. The Fae were in tune with nature, and all of its creatures. They would never harm anything for sport. The animals knew this.

When she heard nothing else, she took a deep breath to calm her nerves and set out again. A large tree trunk appeared in her path, and Bitsy sidestepped to go around it.

A large palm clamped down over her mouth, stifling her scream as a powerful arm wrapped around her body and Bitsy was yanked backward into a hard, warm chest.

"Did I, or did I not, tell you to wait in the goddamn truck?"

The words were growled in her ear. It was so cold she could see his breath. Her heart pounded even as her body went slack with relief. Spots danced in front of her eyes, and she realized he was holding her so tight she couldn't breathe. Bitsy pulled at his hand, and he released her, but immediately grabbed her by the arm.

Bitsy didn't try to get away. Instead, she allowed him to hold it as she bent over, gasping for air. When she could breathe somewhat normally again, she straightened and glared at him. "You scared the hell out of me, you asshole!"

Keegan stuck his face in hers. "How the fuck do you think I felt when I returned to the truck to find you gone?"

Bitsy looked at him. Really looked at him. Rage contorted his handsome features. But beneath it was honest-to-God fear. He'd been truly concerned for her. Something warm and fuzzy filled her chest, and she scowled and yanked her arm from his grasp. "I'm fine."

Keegan scrubbed his face with his hands. He was wearing nothing but his jeans and boots—and his hat, of course. Bitsy's eyes fell of their own accord to his chest, corded with muscle and a light sprinkling of hair. Without thought, she lifted her hand to feel the soft curls beneath her fingertips but jerked her arm back against her body before they made contact with his warm skin.

What the hell am I doing?

"Why did you leave the truck?"

It took her a moment to realize he was speaking to her. Her eyes flew from his pecs to his face. "What?"

"The truck, Bitsy. I told you to stay in the truck until I came back for you."

She almost told him the truth, but something held her back. A test, perhaps, that he would live up to his word. "I just needed to do something besides sit, so I thought a little walk wouldn't hurt."

Hands low on his hips, he tilted his head back and searched the treetops, as though searching the heavens for patience.

Bitsy rolled her eyes at his dramatics, but apparently, he'd found what he was looking for. Because when he looked at her again, his face was calm, the angry twist gone from his mouth.

"And what if someone other than me had found you?"

"They wouldn't."

"No?"

"No."

"Why not?"

"Because I would know they were there before they found me."

"You didn't know *I* was there."

He had a point. But it was only because she'd been distracted by the rabbit. "You got lucky. I was thinking about something else."

"What were you thinking about?" His face was carefully composed as he waited for her answer.

She pressed her lips together. Let him think what he wanted.

But he just sighed as his eyes searched her face. "All right, ittybit. Let's get back to the truck and get camp set up. Merrick wants us gone by sundown tomorrow."

"What if we don't find anything by then?" Horrible thoughts ran through her head. What if her father was being held here against his will? Not all Fae got along. He might've run into someone who had a grudge against him. It would explain why he hadn't come to Seattle yet.

And if Faeries didn't want to be found, it wouldn't be easy to do so. It could take weeks or months. Even for her.

"It was the best I could do," he told her, and she heard a thread of sympathy in his voice. "We'll do what we can. Hopefully, we can at least find out if your father is here."

Bitsy nodded, not knowing what else to say without giving away her secret.

"Okay, then. Let's go." He turned to lead the way back to the truck.

Four long, bloody claw marks slashed open the skin of his back from shoulder to rib. She must've gasped out loud, for he glanced back over his shoulder, his brows drawn together in question.

"What happened to your back?"

One side of his mouth lifted in something between a smile and a grimace. "Nothing to worry about, ittybit. Just a normal greeting between rival Alphas. It'll heal." He waved his hand over his nude torso. "But, yeah. I didn't want to get blood on my shirt." He reached back and took her hand. "Come on."

She let him pull her along, her eyes on the ugly slashes, not sure how to interpret the emotions jumbled up inside of her.

Bitsy's concern was touching, but Keegan wasn't foolish enough to believe it would soften her opinion of him. Honestly, he was surprised he'd gotten off as easy as he had with Merrick, all things considered. The Colorado Alpha liked to throw his weight around.

When they got back to the truck, he pulled it up to the agreed upon location and started setting up camp, brushing off Bitsy's offer to help. It was cold, and she was still running around in shorts. He could get the tent up faster without her help, and then he'd make a small fire to keep her warm.

Keegan set about his tasks with no need for more light. It was a full moon, and the local wolf pack would be enjoying the hunt deep in the mountains to the west of their camp, which was why they had to stick to this loca-tion until the next day. Even so, Keegan would have to stay vigilant, just in case any wolves strayed over this way.

As the moon rose higher in the clear sky, a shudder

racked through him. He didn't *have* to shift every time there was a full moon, but he sure as hell *wanted* to. As a matter of fact, if he could've done it, he would have postponed this little trip for a day. But Merrick had insisted he come right away, and was a bit put out when Keegan refused his offer to stay at his house.

He heard the first call of the wolves as they began to sing. If he waited until dawn, they would be back at their cabins and crashed out hard for the day, and it would be safe to take Bitsy to search for her father.

As more wolves joined the song, Keegan kept his hands busy, not wanting to delve into the reasons it was so important to find the Fae for her, and also to distract him from the desire to join the others. If he were a younger wolf, the pull of the moon would be near irresistible.

Hell, he was having a hard enough time now.

He leaned down to pound a stake into the ground and nearly fell on his ass when he was pushed out of the way.

Bitsy took the rock from his hand. "I got this. Go find some firewood. It's fucking freezing."

He watched, not quite as shocked as he should be, as she quickly and efficiently pounded the stake into the cold ground and moved on to the next one.

He touched the brim of his hat. "Yes, ma'am."

A few minutes later, he was back with an armful of fallen branches and kindling. While she finished setting up the tent, he lit the kindling and fanned the flames until he had a steady fire going.

When he looked up again, she was standing across from him, holding her hands over the heat. He noticed her legs were red from the cold, but rather than ask her why she didn't just put on a pair of the pants he'd bought her—a move that would surely get him an earful—he just added some more wood. The tent was erected behind her, as well as he could have done it. Maybe better. "Are you hungry, ittybit?"

She frowned down at him. "Why do you call me that?"

"Isn't it obvious?"

She didn't respond.

"If you don't like it, I'll try to stop." He grinned. "But I ain't promising you anything."

After a moment, she shook her head. "No. It's okay."

Her easy capitulation surprised him. "So, how about some food? I don't know about you, but I'm starving." Other than a few snacks they'd picked up when they stopped for gas, neither of them had eaten since that morning.

"What about your back?"

"Ah, it'll be fine." He planned to pour some water over the scratches and scrub them clean with his dirty shirt once he'd filled his belly.

"It doesn't look fine."

"It'll be healed by morning."

She rolled her eyes. "How about you stop the tough guy façade and let me clean you up because I don't want you getting blood all over everything? Especially since you're forcing me to share your tent."

Keegan bit back a laugh at the sour look on her face. Her bedside manner could use a little improvement, but he yielded the argument to her. "I would appreciate that. Thank you, ittybit." He pointed with his chin toward the truck behind her. "There's a first aid kit in the truck behind the drivers' seat." His skin was fair twitching at the thought of her touching him of her own free will, tenderly cleaning his wounds.

Without another word, she went to go get the kit and brought it back over to the fire. "Sit," she ordered, and pointed to a flat rock wide enough to work as a chair.

Keegan swallowed hard. On second thought, maybe this wasn't such a good idea.

Bitsy cocked her head and tapped her foot.

With a deep breath, he sat. Pulling his knees up, he wrapped his arms around his legs and stared into the flames as he listened to her rummaging around in the box behind him. Her touch, when it finally came, was gentle but firm on his skin. Her skin was soft, just as he'd imagined it.

Her warm fingertips touched the base of his neck, and a shiver raced down his spine. It didn't hurt at all, and he closed his eyes as she probed gently at the wound.

"This might sting a bit," she said softly in his ear.

Fire burned a trail down his back.

Keegan jerked, his body arching forward as he automatically tried to escape the pain of the alcohol. "Son of a bitch!"

"Sorry. I warned you."

He grunted in response. She didn't sound sorry. She sounded downright gleeful about it all. "You didn't need to do that. I'm a werewolf. I don't get infections."

"Well, you can never be too careful."

Her touch left him for a moment, and he tensed when it returned. But she only dabbed at his wounds with a soft cloth. After a minute, Keegan relaxed again, and let her administer to his wounds with no more complaints.

All too soon, she was finished. "There," she told him softly. "All done."

He stretched his muscles, feeling the tightness of his healing wounds and the tape holding the gauze over the worst of them. He looked back over his shoulder. Her small face was only inches from his. "Thank you," he told her sincerely.

Her eyes, dark and soulful as a gypsy, danced away. "You're welcome." She put the supplies back in the kit and closed it up. "I'll take that food now. I'm starving."

Keegan grinned. "Yes, ma'am." Within a few minutes, he had hot dogs and beans cooking over the fire.

Bitsy wrinkled her nose. "I don't eat the random guts of pigs. Or cows, for that matter."

"Well, that's good," Keegan told her. "Because these are vegan dogs." Pulling the sticks from the fire, he checked the beans and walked to the truck to find the buns.

"Aren't you cold?"

He didn't have to look to know her eyes were on his chest as he returned to the fire. He could feel the heat of her gaze on his bare skin. They branded him as deep as a hot iron, like he was her property. The feeling wasn't unpleasant. Besides, his shirt was still in the back of the truck. He'd figured he'd put it on after his wounds had healed more and he had a chance to wash up. "Nope. Us wolves run hot."

"That's the understatement of the year."

The words were muttered under her breath, but he still heard them. Keegan cocked an eyebrow. "If my manly chest is too distracting for you, I'd be more than happy to cover it up."

She gave a very unladylike snort. "Is that food done, yet?"

Keegan handed her a dog and scooped some beans into a metal camping bowl for her. Wordlessly, he got his own grub and went to sit beside her.

She gave him some side-eye but didn't otherwise protest his nearness. They ate in silence, and when they were done, he took her bowl and set it aside to wash before they went to sleep. An owl hooted in the distance, but other than the crackling fire, the night was quiet.

Keegan glanced up at the moon, rising higher in the sky. The wolves must be deep into the hunt by now. He rubbed the back of his neck, easing the tension. Between the urge to run and this female sharing his tent, he'd be lucky to get any sleep at all tonight.

"Why do you do it?" Her voice was tiny.

He didn't need to ask her to what she was referring. "That's a hard question to answer, ittybit."

She looked right at him then, and her eyes were black as ink in her white face. "Try."

Explain to her something he didn't quite understand himself? It was a lot to ask. Breathing deep, he took in her scent. It filled his lungs, fusing with the oxygen in his blood until it became a part of him. "I have a better idea. Dance with me."

"There's no music."

"We don't need any."

"I want you to answer my question."

Still stubborn as all get out. "If I answer it, will you dance with me?"

She scowled at him. "Why the hell do you want to dance in the middle of the wilderness with no music?"

Because he needed something to keep his mind off the full moon, and off the desire to run free and wild beneath it. And having her lush, little body in his arms would be just the thing. "Humor me."

Indecision battled plainly on her face, but in the end, she heaved a great sigh. "Fine. I'll dance with you. If you put a shirt on, and if you answer my question."

"Agreed. The answer to your question is—" He paused and scratched the back of his neck. "I don't know."

"You don't know?"

"I don't know." He glanced over at her. "Well, that's not exactly true. I guess I do know why I started hunting Fae for the rodeo."

She moved a bit closer to the fire and gave him her full attention.

"A few of us found those two soul suckers one night while we were out hunting, and Jace had the bright idea to bring them back to the old barn. The pack, well, let's just say things hadn't exactly been peaceful between us here since the end of the war, so I allowed it. We had some iron chains to hold them, but the other building—the one you were in—wasn't built yet."

He scrubbed his face with his hands. He hadn't shaved since that morning, and the stubble made it itch. "I don't even remember whose idea it was to use them for entertainment. Maybe it was mine, I honestly don't know. But the rest of the pack perked right up when I gave them a purpose. They started throwing ideas out right and left, and eventually it was decided we were going to build us a rodeo." He looked at her then. "It was the first thing in a long time that brought some life into the pack. It gave them a purpose. Gave them a reason for existing. Other packs, like Merrick's here, heard what was going on, and we invited them to come see what we were doing. I charge them a fee to be let in, and a fee to compete if they wanted. I know to you it sounds like a horrible thing, but it gave us another stream of income. And more importantly, it brought packs together. It brought *my* pack together. It gave some meaning to lives that were otherwise drifting through the days, bored and restless. It did a lot of good things."

"Why couldn't you just plant a garden? Take up knitting?"

The image of a bunch of macho males gathered around the sitting room clicking their needles with a roll of yarn at their feet almost made him laugh out loud. "Wolves are pack animals, and so are werewolves. The pack works together. Lives together. They do every-thing together. A wolf without a pack won't last very long, and those that do are some hard ass mother fuckers."

"You're not telling me anything I don't already know."

"If the pack has nothing to do, no territory to protect, no prey to hunt, they'll start fighting amongst themselves. Or, they'll go looking for territory to steal. Or, worse, they'll go searching for prey." He ran his fingers through his hair. "In this case, it was either let them hunt the Fae, or take the chance they would start hunting humans."

"Because humans are more important than my people?"

"No, ittybit. That's not what I'm saying."

"Then what the hell *are* you saying, Keegan? Because that's exactly what it sounded like to me."

His voice rose to match hers, his patience at an end. He was trying to explain, and she wasn't listening. "Dammit, Bitsy. Stop making me out to be a monster."

She stood and stomped over to the other side of the fire before she spun around, pinning him where he was with the hatred spewing from her eyes. "You ARE a fucking monster. You almost killed my mother in your sick little sport!"

Keegan stood also. "That was not me, Bitsy."

"You didn't stop it!" she screamed at him.

He took a step back. She was right. He didn't stop it. He didn't stop any of it. Instead, he'd averted his eyes when Bitsy was in the ring, finding some reason or another to start a conversation with whoever was standing closest to him. Like the fucking coward he was.

"You allowed your pack to do whatever the hell they wanted to us. Break our bones! Drag us through the dirt with an iron chain around our necks until there was no skin on our backs! You even put us in the ring with the soul suckers! Do you know what would've happened if they'd managed to get to one of us?"

He did know.

Shame heated his neck and chest. He didn't know what to say. There was nothing he *could* say. He didn't know what he'd been thinking, asking her to come back here, thinking he could somehow make things up to her.

A single tear escaped and trailed down her cheek. The telltale sign of emotion broke the tension, and she deflated before him, her entire body seeming to crumble in on itself.

"Ittybit." He reached for her across the fire, not feeling the searing heat, and probably would have walked through it to hold her if she'd let him.

A howl rent the air. It was close, too close, and Keegan froze. It had come from the trees behind Bitsy.

Her eyes flew to his, and she reached for him. Her small hand shook violently. He could only imagine the PTSD she must have.

Keegan caught and held her eyes with his, his arm still outstretched over the fire. He took a step, nearly in the flames.

A growl sounded from the trees, even closer now.

Bitsy turned to look behind her.

A pair of glowing yellow eyes stared back.

"Bitsy. Listen to me." Keegan stepped to the side, slowly making his way around the fire to her, his eyes on the large werewolf not fifty feet away. His voice was low, calming, even as his body shuddered, itching to shift and face this threat. "Do not run. Do you hear me? Do NOT run." He was almost within touching distance of her.

Bitsy glanced at him. Her features were frozen in fear.

Then she spun on her heel and ran.

CHAPTER 9

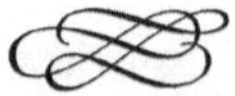

Bitsy ran for her life, her open coat flapping behind her. If any humans had been camping nearby, they would've seen something resembling a large, drunken butterfly darting through the forest. She heard Keegan yell after her, just before she heard a roar the likes of which she'd never heard before, but she kept running.

She knew what would happen to her if that wolf caught her. That thing wasn't just curious about the fire or the raised voices. It was in full hunting mode, just like Keegan's wolves had been when they'd caught her and her mom. If it caught her, she'd be captured.

Or, perhaps, eaten.

The fall of heavy paws sounded behind her, gaining speed. Bitsy dodged a large tree trunk, pumping her arms and legs as hard as they would go. She tried to reach out to her father, to feel his presence as she had before, to go to him, but there was nothing but the pounding of her heart and the icy chill of fear.

There was a grunt of breath, and something brushed her shoulder as a large blur of white went flying over her head. The wolf landed in front of her, reared up, and spun around on its back legs to cut her off.

Bitsy hit the ground, sliding like a ball player coming in on a home run. Except there was no base to stop her, and she slid right under the belly of the beast. Scrambling to her hands and knees, she tried to crawl out from beneath it.

A large paw landed on her back and pressed her to the ground as a low growl raised the hair on the back of her neck. Goosebumps rose all over her body, and out of the corner of her eye she saw teeth. Long, white, very sharp teeth.

Son of a bitch.

But instead of the bite she expected, the wolf lowered its body over hers, head hung low until they were nearly cheek-to-cheek. Soft fur brushed her temple as it stared off into the trees. Something hard and cold touched the side of her neck.

Her necklace.

Her breath whooshed out as her entire body relaxed, and Bitsy looked, too. The grey wolf from the forest paced back and forth about twenty feet in front of them, its glowing eyes never leaving her. Which meant the beast on top of her was Keegan.

He was protecting her. Like Marc did Bronaugh when he'd broken them out of the rodeo. A werewolf only had the instinct to do this when it was protecting one of its pack.

Or its mate.

"Oh, *hell* no." The words came out before she could stop them. Slapping a hand over her mouth, she tried to sink into the frost-covered leaves that were, even now, soaking through her shirt and shorts to freeze every inch of her skin. Guess "weather resistant" didn't mean weather proof. But the two wolves paid her no mind, busy as they were seeing who had the bigger dick.

From previous interactions, Bitsy would guess it was Keegan.

Keegan's weight left her as he lifted his large head and howled. His wolf song reverberated through his warm body and into hers, and she covered her ears with her hands to protect her eardrums. Then he lowered his large chest over her again.

Bitsy turned her head slightly and glanced at him out of the corner of her eye. His muzzle was lifted in a snarl, and those long canines glistened directly beside her head.

It became very clear he was claiming her.

The other wolf paused its pacing. Its large grey face swung from one side to the other, weighing its choices. Faced with a threat like this, Bitsy assumed it would tuck tail and run, but the idiot decided to ignore the warning signs and took a cautious step forward.

Keegan tensed above her and growled low in his throat.

Time stood still as Bitsy waited to see what the other wolf would do. Her nose began to run a little from the cold, and she wiggled it. It didn't help much, but she dared not move her arm, even if she could.

She kept her eyes on the other wolf. It stood frozen— ears up, tail straight, its yellow eyes staring right at

Keegan. Ripples of tension traveled over her skin. It wasn't backing away from the Alpha above her as it should. It wasn't showing any signs of submission at all. This couldn't be good.

Unable to ignore her running nose any longer, Bitsy sniffed, and the world exploded around her.

Crisp, cold air rushed over her legs and back as Keegan and the other wolf lunged at each other without warning. At least, not one that she could see. They collided mid-air, and the strange wolf cried out as Keegan caught him on the shoulder with his massive jaws. They landed in a twist of fur and teeth, each one scrambling for the upper position.

And they were coming closer and closer to her spot in the leaves.

Without thinking about it, Bitsy got to her feet and reached for the nearest branch. She scaled the tree, ignoring the bark scraping her hands and legs, until she was high enough to stay out of the way. Once up there, she found a sturdy place to sit and pulled her coat tight against the cold. The tree, ancient and wise, embraced her with its leaves, its old soul a reassuring presence.

In retrospect, she wondered if running away would have been the smarter thing to do. What if Keegan didn't win? However, it soon became clear to her she had no worries in that regard. Her wolf was kicking the other wolf's ass, and she had to admit she could see exactly why it was he was Alpha.

Something else became apparent to her. Keegan was holding back, playing defense, not offense. After the initial wrestling match, both wolves got to their feet and faced off. Whenever the other wolf would have a go at him, Keegan would knock him back with a well-placed bite or swipe of his large paw, but he didn't go in for the kill. Even when the other wolf was staggering from a particularly hard blow to the head, clearly wounded. Even when the smell of blood was so strong, the bloodlust had to be running high.

Still, he held back.

Bitsy didn't know many males in her world—especially not shifters—who had that kind of self-control.

The fight was winding down. Keegan showed little signs of exertion, other than his heaving sides and the blood dripping from his muzzle.

As the other wolf finally called it and staggered off with its head down and its tail tucked between its legs, just as she had imagined, Bitsy jumped down out of the tree. She gave the trunk a quick hug, murmuring her thanks. Keegan's head swung around at the sudden sound of her boots crunching through the leaves, and his big body gave a great, shuddering sigh and relaxed upon seeing her.

"Is it gone?"

An eerie light glowed from behind his green eyes, giving them a slightly yellow hue. They lingered on her body as Bitsy brushed the dirt, leaves, and pine needles away, and tried to rub some warmth back into her frozen thighs. She didn't need to look to know he was watching her. She could feel his eyes.

She straightened, and he turned and started back to camp. When she didn't follow him right away, his large head swung around to check on her, and her necklace glinted in the moonlight, pulled snug around his neck.

She pulled her coat tighter and followed him.

Keegan remained on high alert all the way back to camp. His large paws made less noise than an animal half his size as he picked through the underbrush, eyes shifting from side to side, his ears cocked for any sound.

"I'm sorry," she told him when the fire was in sight. "For running. It was a gut reaction. After what happened to me last time," she added under her breath.

A gruff exhale was her only response.

When they got back to camp, Bitsy put more wood on the fire while Keegan patrolled the perimeter, his nose low to the ground, checking for any signs of their intruder. When the circle was complete, he went behind the truck and Bitsy heard his grunts of pain and heavy breathing as he shifted back.

She couldn't imagine why anyone would want to do that to themselves voluntarily. Though she supposed that's why they "ran hot." The saying didn't just pertain to body temperature, though that was also true. Wolves, like vampires or any other supernatural creature, were victims of their hot-blooded natures.

Keegan came back to her wimpy fire, his shirt in one hand and carrying his boots and hat with the other. Blood streaked his torso, and he had a gash above his right eye.

"You're hurt." Bitsy jumped to her feet to get the first aid kit, but his icy tone stopped her in her tracks.

"I'm fine." He put on his boots, then went to the tent. He came out with a canteen and his dirty shirt from earlier. Wetting one corner, he wiped the blood from his skin. "We're leaving at first light."

Bitsy wasn't put off by his surliness. "To go where?"

"Home."

"What about the lead on my father?"

He grimaced as he cleaned off one of the deeper wounds from the other wolf's claws but didn't answer her.

She clenched her fists at her sides to keep her voice civil. "Keegan? What about my father?"

He glanced up at her, taking in her angry posture. Then he sighed. "It ain't happening, ittybit. I'm sorry."

"That's not acceptable to me."

"That's how it is, darlin'. I suggest you get used to the idea." He threw his bloody shirt into the fire. "Get some sleep. I'll keep watch." Pulling a thermal shirt over his head, he stuck his hat on his head and pulled the brim low, hiding behind it.

But Bitsy would not be put off that easily. This was her father they were talking about. Her family. "Don't you *dare* dismiss me," she hissed at him. "I'm not one of your little puppy dogs."

He laughed without humor. "No, ittybit. You certainly are not. My pups would know better than to put us in the position you just did."

Now she was confused. "What are you talking about? I didn't do anything wrong."

He shoved his hat back, and Bitsy took a step back at the fury glowing from his eyes.

"You fucking ran when I told you not to. You made a bad situation worse by activating every goddamned hunting instinct that shifter has. I had to fight him because of you. And now,"—he took a deep breath—"now we have to get the hell out of Merrick's territory."

"Why?"

"Because that wolf I just fucked up was his brother. If I stick around, Merrick will challenge me to avenge his honor, and I'll have to accept. And I might not win. Merrick isn't known for playing fair. And I have no one here to back me up."

"You have me." The words came out of nowhere. But once they were out there, she realized she meant them. If it would help her get her dad back, she would help him. She wasn't powerless. As long as they kept any iron away from her. Which was highly unlikely.

Keegan shook his head. "You don't get it." He scrubbed at his face, then took a deep breath and leveled her with his steady gaze. "They didn't even know you were here. Not until now, that is."

Bitsy's cheek was vibrating. Something tickled her nose, and she tried to lift her arm to scratch it, but it appeared to be stuck.

She cracked open one eye and lifted her head. Dawn was just breaking the horizon, and with her Fae vision, it lit up the tent well enough. Keegan's bare chest was laid out before her, much like an all-you-can-eat, Texas-sized buffet. His chest hair tickled her chin. One muscular arm held her tight against his side, and the other arm crossed his middle and his large hand rested lightly on her hip. Her right arm was trapped between them, the other was thrown over his lean waist. One leg was hiked up over his.

Bitsy groaned and put her head back down. She'd gone into the tent shortly after he'd informed her they were leaving, but she hadn't meant to fall asleep. She'd meant to fake it until she could sneak the hell out of here.

But it wasn't too late. Slowly and carefully, she disentangled her limbs. The sleeping bag slipped down as she rolled away from him, revealing the ripple of abs, a lean hip, and toned thigh. She froze and contemplated pulling it the rest of the way down.

For it was very clear to her that Keegan slept in the buff. A buff she would very much like to see again.

Then she scolded herself. This *asshat* had done horrible things to her and her family. Well, maybe not directly, but he didn't stop it from happening, either. And he could have stopped it.

And yet, here she was, eyeing him up like she hadn't eaten in a month.

Heart pounding—and not just from the fear of getting caught—she crab-walked over him beneath the sleeping bag. She tried hard not to look down, she really did. And she nearly succeeded, but not quite.

Arms braced on either side of his head, her eyes drifted over his face, and she had the sudden urge to rub her cheek against his new growth of beard like a cat. She looked lower, over the hard expanse of chest muscle covered by soft, curly hairs, down to the concave of his stomach, and then further still, to the shadows between his hips.

Sucking in her breath, she jerked her head up and rolled so she ended up on her back on the other side of him. Exposed to the cold, her skin was soon covered in goose bumps, even beneath the thermal underwear she'd put on before she fell asleep.

Without looking, she carefully reached over and grabbed the corner of the sleeping bag, pulling it toward her until it covered him sufficiently. Then she sat up, shoved her feet into her socks and boots, and glanced over at him one last time.

His soft snores went on without a hitch.

Bitsy unzipped the tent, slow and easy, just far enough that she could squeeze out. Slinging her pack over her shoulder, she peeked back through the opening. When there was no change in his breathing or any other indicator he was waking up, she quietly zipped the tent shut.

A blackbird greeted her from an overhanging branch, and Bitsy silently wished it a happy morning. She started to walk away, then stopped.

Turning, she grinned at her new bird friend, and threw a few suggestions its way. They were, perhaps, a bit spiteful, but completely deserved as far as she was concerned.

CHAPTER 10

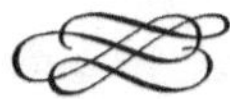

Keegan jerked awake and sat up. The first rays of the sun were bright inside the small tent but were doing little to radiate any heat this early in the morning. Rubbing his palms together to create some friction, he looked over to make sure Bitsy was covered.

And found a whole lot of no Faerie in his sleeping bag.

His immediate reaction was to panic, but he forced himself to stop and take a breath. She probably just needed some privacy. He stretched his arms above his head, then twisted his torso until he felt a satisfying pop in the middle of his spine. No need to worry until there was something worth worrying about.

At least, not until he noticed her bag was also missing.

But still, she could've taken it with her because her clothes were in there.

Throwing off the sleeping bag, he unzipped the tent and stuck his head out. "Bitsy!" A blackbird squawked in response and took off from the tree limb overhanging the campsite, but not before it left a huge gift on his truck on the way out. "Ahh…really?"

He watched as it ran right down the center of his back windshield.

"Son of a bitch." He yanked the tent flap closed. His pants were in the bottom of the bag where he'd kicked them off the night before. It was just too damn uncomfortable trying to sleep in those things. He found them and shoved his feet into the legs, then yanked them up over his hips as he hopped out of the tent. "Bitsy!"

The fire had burned down to warm coals. There was no sign of her anywhere. She'd even stolen his favorite canteen from where he'd left it against a rock the night before.

"Shit…shit!"

How the hell had she snuck out on him? A quick sniff confirmed Merrick's brother hadn't come back, and no one else had come nosing around in the time it took for the moon to fall behind the trees, so he'd assumed they were safe. At least for the moment. And he'd really needed some sleep before the long drive back to Austin. Though he was positive Merrick's brother would go crying to him about what happened first chance he got, the pack would be exhausted after their night of running and hunting.

Bitsy had been sound asleep when he'd finally crawled in with her just a few hours before dawn, and she'd curled around him and stuck to his body like a bur as he'd fallen asleep. Not that he'd minded in the least. Logically, he knew it was because she'd been trying to keep warm. And maybe he was a fool to hope it was anything more than that. But maybe, just maybe, she longed for him like he did her, and she could only show it when she was unconscious.

It was a start. And at this point, he'd take what he could get.

Keegan finished getting dressed. Then he packed up the campsite in record time, double-checked for trash, and threw it all into the backseat of his truck. He'd sort it out later. Once he made sure the fire was covered, he found Bitsy's trail.

She was headed straight toward Merrick's den.

His hackles raised, a sense of foreboding skating over the back of his neck and down his spine, and Keegan set off after her.

He'd make better time if he shifted but shifting without provocation took a lot out of a wolf, and he wanted to save his energy. He had a feeling he was going to need it. Besides, he could tell from her tracks she was walking at a brisk pace, but there was no evidence she was in distress.

Following her trail, Keegan upped his pace to a jog, stopping every now and again to bend down and make sure he hadn't lost her trail.

What the hell was she thinking? Taking off like this? It's not like she didn't know what the stakes were if she was caught, and it's not like she didn't know how dangerous it was because he'd told her. She was a smart female. She wouldn't take off like this without a damn good reason.

But she had a good reason. She had a great reason. Her dad.

All Keegan could hope was that he would find her before Merrick or one of his pack did.

Around a copse of trees, her tracks changed direction, veering off course and picking up speed. Keegan's heart gave a heavy thump when he saw more tracks join hers.

He followed the group to a stream. And the trail went cold.

Without pause, he slogged through the shallow, icy water to the opposite bank. There was nothing on the other side—not a partial print, nothing. Just to be sure, he walked up and down the bank four times.

Keegan swallowed down the panic. Faeries were fast. Maybe even faster than werewolves. There was a chance she hit the water and lost them.

But which way would she have gone?

There was no way to know for sure. But he could find out if she'd been caught, and to do that he'd have to go back to Merrick's. Of course, if he showed up, there was a one hundred percent chance he wouldn't get one boot in the door before he was thrown into a fight to avenge his brother's honor. He wouldn't get the chance or the time to sniff around for Bitsy. He hadn't been lying about that. It was the way of wolves.

Keegan bent down and splashed some cold water on his face, then stared into the clear water, hoping it would tell him what to do. But of course, no answer was forthcoming. He'd always planned to make amends with Merrick over what happened. He was just gonna have to bite the bullet a little sooner than planned. It was the only way to make sure she was safe.

Mind made up, Keegan followed the stream to the next

rise and then turned east toward Merrick's home. It took him less than thirty minutes to find the small cluster of cabins. Not surprisingly, Merrick's was the largest, set smack dab in the middle of the others. But as considerable in size as it was, it wasn't immediately noticeable unless you knew what you were looking for. Unlike Keegan's own home, this pack preferred to blend in with the forest around them as much as possible. And that included their homes.

Walking right up to his front door, Keegan rapped loudly. The only way to do this was to be a male and face what had happened the night before straight on. He was an Alpha. And he wasn't a pussy. He'd own up to what happened, and his part in it. He'd just hoped to do it once he'd gotten Bitsy safely back to Austin. The fight hadn't been his idea. He'd tried to avoid it. And even while it was happening, he'd gone as easy as he could on the cocky little shit. Hopefully, that would count for something.

But he had his priorities, and Bitsy's safety was right up there on that list. It always had been, and not just since she'd come back to him, whether or not she chose to believe it.

Merrick's scent came to him first—a whiff of prime-aged wolf tinged with the stench of someone who grew up with everything money could offer. A direct contrast to the way the pack leader chose to live these days. The heavy wooden door opened slowly to reveal a nude male about Keegan's height with bloodshot eyes, dark, messy hair and a short, well-groomed beard. Hard and wiry, smaller than most other shifters, and with his nerdy look, the Colorado pack master was often mistaken as someone others thought they could push around, but they quickly learned otherwise if they dared to challenge him. And he had the stare to prove it—kind of distant, yet razor sharp, with a touch of fatigue and a dash of cockiness.

However, Keegan knew better than to test the other Alpha. He and Merrick had had a friendly rivalry going on for quite a few years now. He respected the neighboring Alpha, and hoped Merrick felt the same way about him.

Still, rules were rules.

"Keegan." Merrick glanced past him, scanning the forest that surrounded the cabin before his attention came back to his guest. "I suppose you've come here to apologize."

Not quite the greeting he'd been expecting. "I've come to explain what happened," Keegan corrected him.

Merrick blocked the doorway, in full view of the world outside, obviously uncaring about who saw him in his state of undress. Most shifters didn't. Nudity was something you got comfortable with real quick. After a pause, Merrick stepped back and held the door open.

The only thing Keegan could hear was the blood rushing through his head, yet at the same time, the sound of his boots when they hit the hard floor sounded as loud as gunshots. As soon as he stepped inside, Keegan was jolted alert. The slightest scent of moonflowers wafted through the air, yet there wasn't a vase in sight. Or any fresh cut flowers, for that matter. Which meant Bitsy was here somewhere. Or at least, she had been at some point. And not very long ago.

But was Merrick aware she'd been in his house? He'd smell her, sure. Just like Keegan did. But unless he'd caught a whiff of her during a rodeo event, he wouldn't recognize the scent. Keegan hadn't even noticed, not with the other smells in the barn overpowering her natural scent.

But if Merrick was the one who'd brought her here, then he also knew Keegan would come here looking for her. Yet, he just invited him into his home. So, his fellow Alpha either didn't know Bitsy had been rummaging around while he was sleeping, or he was a real good actor.

Had she really broken into a werewolf's home and nosed around while he was in the next room sleeping? That was the question. And Keegan knew the answer. That female had balls. Larger than any male he knew, including himself.

It wouldn't surprise him in the least.

"Let me go grab some pants," Merrick told him.

Despite his unthreatening demeanor, Keegan kept his guard up. Merrick was being entirely too calm about all of this. Down in Texas, the other shifter wouldn't have made it twenty miles across the border before a challenge was issued to avenge the offended member of the pack.

Keegan wandered into the living area to wait. Large overstuffed furniture took up much of the room, arranged around a fireplace big enough for a man to stand in. A throw rug with a southwest design done in blues and browns covered the bare floor. One wall was made up entirely of built-in bookshelves. There was no television, no pool table, no bar. Only books. Shelves and shelves of books.

Merrick came back into the room. He'd thrown on a

pair of flannel pajama pants and dark-rimmed glasses. "Would you like a beer?"

"Nah, I'm good. But, thanks."

After getting one for himself, Merrick joined Keegan in the living room and invited him to sit.

Keegan leaned forward and braced his elbows on his knees. "How is Stan?" He didn't bother trying to hide the concern he felt. There was no need to play tough guy, and though he didn't have much respect for the younger wolf, he had a hell of a lot for his older brother.

Merrick ran his thumb around the open mouth of the bottle. "He's fine. No harm done. Other than to his pride. Which we both know could use a few more hits. Oh, and one tooth will probably need to be replaced."

He smiled, and it was genuine. Keegan bowed his head a moment. "I tried to avoid fighting him. But the little shit just wouldn't give it up. I did what I had to do, but only enough to send him runnin' back home."

"You don't have to explain, Keegan. I know how my brother is. He likes to push the boundaries, especially when he's hunting. He didn't get anything he didn't deserve."

Keegan kept his features carefully impassive.

"Stan thinks rules are to be broken, and when he's in his other form, the most primitive part of his brain completely takes over. There's not an ounce of common sense in there. He's impulsive, and untrustworthy. And if he wasn't my brother, he would be dead by now." Lifting the beer to his lips, Merrick took a deep drink. "If anything, I actually owe *you* an apology. He was told to stay on this side of the mountain and away from your campsite. He disobeyed a direct order."

Keegan watched for any telltale signs that he was pulling his leg, but Merrick was either telling the truth or he was slippery as grease. "I tried not to hurt him too bad."

"Thank the gods you have more control than my rambunctious little brother."

An uncomfortable silence descended upon the room. Merrick had given him no reason to think otherwise, but something was telling Keegan all was not as it seemed.

"Don't worry, my friend," Merrick leaned forward and put his hand on Keegan's knee. "All is well between us. You can remove that furrow from your brow." He slapped Keegan's knee once and stood. "Are you sure you don't want a beer?"

"No, thank you."

"Well, let me get one and then you can catch me up on the latest news from Texas."

Keegan stood as well. "Actually, Merrick, I really need to get going. I still have that 'livestock' to try to catch today, and wanna follow up that lead you gave me."

Merrick spoke over his shoulder as he went into the kitchen. "I'm surprised you came alone. Doesn't Jace normally handle this kind of thing?" He got another beer from the fridge and popped the cap off. He smiled. "Oh wait, that's right. Jace is dead."

Merrick had been there the night it had all gone down, and Keegan had to wonder what he was playing at.

Leaning back against the counter, Merrick crossed his arms over his bare chest and took another long drink, wiping his mouth with his forearm. "Stone, then. Why isn't Stone handling this?"

"Stone wasn't available." Keegan kept his answer short and sweet. Merrick was fishing, and he wasn't about to give him anything to sink his hook into. "Plus, I didn't think you'd be keen on a bunch of wolves that don't belong to you tromping around your territory."

Merrick smiled, but it didn't quite reach his eyes. "You would be right." He drank the remainder of his second beer down in three big swallows and set the empty bottle on the counter. "I'll expect you gone by sundown."

"That's the deal." Keegan took his opportunity to leave. The tension in the room was building, and he wanted to get while the gettin' was good. He gave Merrick a nod. "I'll let myself out." At the door, he turned. "Thanks again for this. Everyone will appreciate having some new entertainment if this lead pans out."

"I'm looking forward to it myself."

Stepping outside, Keegan squinted into the brisk sunshine and went to adjust his hat down over his eyes, before realizing he'd forgotten to grab it out of the truck.

CHAPTER 11

Bitsy sat in the corner of the dark cabin and pulled up her pant leg. She eyed the iron shackle around her ankle with distaste. They'd been smart enough to remove her boots and socks before they'd shackled her so she couldn't slip out of it, but that hadn't stopped her from trying to rip it off, and now she was shackled *and* bleeding. At least Keegan had given them their own cell to stay in. These guys were amateurs.

Which didn't mean she could get out of the shackle, however.

Of all the things that could cause weakness in a Faerie, why did it have to be a type of metal? Why couldn't it be something like daisies? Daisies she could walk away from. Or pluck.

Her father's aura was moving farther and farther away. Bitsy felt it, like a radio signal getting weaker and weaker. But he'd been here, or nearby. She'd followed his Faerie call to a creek. By then she was being followed by a scraggly group of shifters—Merrick's, she assumed—and hoped they would lead her straight to her father.

Or bring her to him, as the case may be.

So, she'd allowed them to "catch" her. These young ones weren't near as wily as Keegan's pack. She'd never seen his guys coming until she was caught up in their trap, her mom beside her, looking at each other in complete and utter shock. But she practically had to stand still and wave her arms for Merrick's guys to find her.

In the end, it had all been for nothing. Her dad wasn't here. The closer they'd gotten to Merrick's den, the weaker his signal had gotten. She'd placed her bet, and she'd lost.

Now, she just needed to figure out a way out of here. It shouldn't be too hard, if her interaction with these assholes up until now were any indication.

The door creaked open and a young boy stuck his head around the corner. Round brown eyes skittered around the interior before landing on her.

Bitsy smiled at the kid. He was adorable.

He eyed her with distrust for a few seconds, but finally screwed up his courage and came inside, pushing the door closed with his skinny hip. There was a plate in his hand with what looked like lunchmeat piled high in the center.

Maybe these guys weren't as lame as she'd originally thought. Perhaps they knew what they were doing, sending in a kid. They probably hoped they'd tap into her maternal instincts, and they were right. Bitsy would never hurt a child.

"Hey, kiddo." She nodded at the plate in his hand. "If that's dead animal carcass on there, you can tell your big, bad wolf leader thanks, but no thanks." She waved him back out the door as he stood there, unsure of what to do. "As a matter of fact, just go ahead and take that away. It smells disgusting."

"But I was told to make sure you eat it," he told her.

She felt bad for the kid, she really did. But nothing—absolutely fucking nothing—would make her swallow the processed crap on that plate. Even if it wasn't loosely made of an innocent animal. "Ain't happening, hon. Sorry."

The door creaked behind the kid, and Bitsy leaned to the side so she could see around his thin body.

Keegan stuck his head inside, much as the child had. Only his eyes weren't skittish at all. They were narrowed with determination.

"About time you got here," she told him. "Would you please tell this child there is no way in hell I'm going to eat the stuff on that plate?"

After checking over his shoulder to make no one had seen him, Keegan stepped inside and closed the door behind him.

The boy stared up at him with such an expression of terror it was almost comical.

With a smile, Keegan ruffled his dark blond hair. "You can't feed Faeries meat, kid. They'd starve before they'd eat one of nature's creatures."

The kid finally found his voice. "What do you feed them, then?"

"Fruits, veggies, pasta, bread—"

"Can we save the feeding Faeries lesson for later and get me the fuck out of here?" Bitsy cut in.

Keegan frowned. "Language."

He sounded like her mother, and she gave him the same response she would give her. She rolled her eyes.

Eyeing her shackle, he said, "Did I, or did I not tell you not to leave camp?"

He had to be kidding. He was going to give her a lecture on her behavior *now*? "Technically, you just told me we had to leave Merrick's territory by morning. You didn't tell me, specifically, not to leave camp before then."

For a moment, she almost thought he was going to leave her there, just to prove his point. But he turned his attention to the boy. "What's your name, son?"

"Brian."

"Brian, do you know where the key is for the chains?"

"No, sir."

"All right. Well, I'm just going to have to break it, then. I'll send Merrick a new one." Sitting on his haunches, he got eye-to-eye with the child. "I'm gonna need you to stay right here. Got it?" His voice vibrated with the timbre of the Alpha.

Brian nodded a little too fast. "Yes, sir."

The poor kid. He didn't have a chance.

Keegan ruffled his hair again and came over to Bitsy. She held her bloody ankle out to him with a smile.

His features went cold as he stared down at it. "They did this to you?"

She glanced at the torn skin. "No. I did this to me trying to get it off. I was about to start chewing when Brian here showed up." She gave the kid a wink.

He almost smiled. Almost.

"Just get it off, please." Tired of holding her foot up, she let it drop to the floor.

Sitting on his heels beside her, Keegan carefully placed her ankle on his jean-clad thigh. He slid his fingers inside the cuff, and Bitsy winced as they rubbed her raw skin. His dark brows drew down so far they nearly swallowed his nose, like it was her fault he'd hurt her. Though, she supposed, in his male mind, it was. If she hadn't run off and gotten herself captured, she wouldn't be chained up, and he wouldn't have to hurt her while trying to "save" her. Little did he know, if he hadn't shown up when he had, she would've gotten herself out of here. Just because she wouldn't hurt a child didn't mean she wouldn't be able to talk him into helping her.

With a quick jerk, he separated the cuff from the chain. "I'll have to get the cuff off later," he told her.

"But, the iron—"

Green eyes bright with anger met hers, shocking her into silence. "I won't let anything happen to you." Then he slid one arm under her knees and the other behind her back, and stood up with her in his arms. "Brian?"

That timbre was back in his voice. It crawled over Bitsy's skin like a thousand little spiders. It was worse than having chills.

"Yes, sir?"

"I'm taking this little lady with me, and I'm gonna need you to stay right here for a good five minutes after we leave. That's three hundred seconds. Can you count for me?"

The boy nodded. "One Mississippi...two Mississippi..."

Keegan nodded. "Good. Keep it up, son."

"Won't he get in trouble?" she asked as he made his way over to the door.

"Nah. Only if he tries to lie to them about what happened. I didn't ask him to lie. Only to give us a head start. They're wolves. They all know it's near impossible not to follow an Alpha's command. Especially for one so young." He shifted her weight until he was holding her in one arm and opened the door a crack. Bitsy wrapped her arms around his neck as he peered out.

"I can walk, you know."

"I know." Yet, he made no move to put her down.

She should be repulsed by his closeness, and it angered her that she wasn't. He smelled great for a guy who'd spent the night in a tent, and every part of him she touched was warm, hard muscle.

Even his messy hair and beard stubble was sexy.

She felt the wall around her heart crack a little more.

No, this wasn't good. She needed space. But before she could wriggle out of his arms, he swung the door open wide and went out onto the small porch. With his back glued to the wall, he sidestepped to the edge and peered around the corner before jumping down and running in a crouch toward the cover of trees.

As soon as they were a safe distance away, Bitsy released her death grip on his neck and squirmed until he had no choice but to set her down on her bare feet. She took a grateful breath of the crisp air.

"You have no shoes." He pointed at her feet for emphasis.

"Very observant of you." Spinning on her bare heel, she

continued walking, ignoring the pain every time the cuff was jostled on her raw ankle.

"Where are you going? The truck is this way."

"I'm not going to the truck."

"Pardon?"

"I'm not going to the truck."

"I heard you the first time."

"Then why did you ask?"

"Bitsy."

She kept walking.

"Bitsy! Dammit! Stop for a second and talk to me." He grabbed her by the upper arm and spun her around.

"What?"

"What do you mean, what? Where the hell are you going?"

She opened her mouth to give him a smartass retort, but then she stopped and took a deep breath. She was tired, she was shackled in iron, and honestly, she could use his help. "My father is here."

Keegan straightened. "How do you know? Did you see him?"

"No." She shook her head. "But I know. He's here. Or, at least, he was."

"Explain."

"We're wasting time." She started walking again.

He fell into step beside her. "You need to tell me what's going on, ittybit. Or how am I supposed to help you?"

Reluctantly, she stopped again and looked up at him.

His eyes were darker now, clouded with emotion, his brow lowered with concern.

She crossed her arms over her chest and looked away.

"My father is somewhere close by. I felt him as soon as we arrived last night."

"What do you mean, you 'felt' him?"

"He's my father. A part of me. Just like the dirt and the trees and the birds." She didn't know how to explain it.

"Why didn't you tell me?"

"Because I don't trust you."

He recoiled at the harsh truth of her words, but after a moment, his shoulders relaxed and his head fell forward. "I guess I deserve that."

"You do." She wasn't going to sugarcoat it to spare his feelings. He'd done some sick fucking things to her and her kind. She hoped he felt guilty. He deserved to feel guilty.

"Is there any way you'll ever forgive me for what I allowed them to do to you?" The words were spoken fast and harsh, like they were torn from his soul.

"No," she said without thought or hesitation.

He searched her face. Looking for what, she didn't know. A kink in her armor? A crack of untruth in her words? They were there, both of those things, if he looked close enough.

But he didn't. He took a step back, and with that small gesture, he created a chasm between them as big as The Grand Canyon.

A shadow fell over his features, and Keegan shook his head. "We can't go look for your father right now. Our five minutes is up. Merrick knows I just snuck back onto his property and broke you out. We need to go. And we need to go now."

"I need to find my father. And you told me you would help me."

"I will help you find your father. I promised, and I don't go back on my promises. And I'll get you both home to Seattle safe and sound. Just not right at this moment."

"And then what?" A thousand butterflies fluttered around in her stomach as she waited for his reply.

"Then I'll go back to my life at the ranch and you can go on with yours."

She exhaled in a rush. "And the rodeo?"

He gave her a tight smile. "We're wasting daylight."

Bitsy wanted to force the answer out of him. Wanted to hear him say it. Needed to hear him say it. Because, somehow, he kept chipping away at the wall she'd erected to protect herself from him.

But he was right. She was wasting time standing here arguing with him. What did she need to hear, anyway? How nothing had changed? How he still planned on running the shit show as soon as found some new Fae to abuse?

No. She didn't need to hear any of it to know it was true.

"Bitsy. This is not the time to do this. If your dad is here, we'll come back for him."

"But he might be gone by then."

"He's been here since y'all were separated. I don't see him suddenly leaving now."

She supposed he was right. "But what if he's in trouble? What if Merrick does have him and is just moving him or something? What if I missed him somehow?"

Keegan was shaking his head before she'd finished

talking. "He doesn't. I searched his entire property before I found you. The only Fae I scented was you. Your dad isn't there or anywhere around those cabins."

Common sense told her he was right. They should leave and come back when they had the element of surprise on their side. She didn't want to start a war between two rival Alphas, not when a member of her family could get caught in the middle of it. Her heart stuttered at the thought, but not because she worried about Keegan. Only because she worried about her father.

She was just so fucking *close*.

"Ittybit, we'll get your dad back. I swear it to you."

She scoffed. "That doesn't mean much to me."

"All right, then. How about this? We need to leave now, but we'll come back—"

"When?"

"Soon. And when we do, you'll have boots on your feet and that iron off your ankle. If we tried to do this right now, and we ran into trouble, you'd be in no position to help."

Bitsy looked away. He was right.

"Bitsy, I'm sorry. But we need to go."

He was sincere. She could see it all over his face. With her heart in her throat, she nodded and let him lead her away.

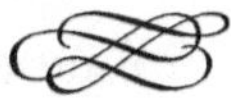

Keegan didn't fully breathe until they were in the truck and on the main road heading back to Austin.

Bitsy sat beside him with her chin in her hand, staring out the window. She hadn't said a word to him since he'd convinced her to leave.

He'd take her back to the hotel and then go get the tools he needed to pry the cuff off her ankle. It would be easier to take her to the ranch, but he wouldn't ask her to go back there.

"Weren't you worried you'd get caught?"

He glanced over at her. She was still staring out the window. "Get caught doing what?"

"Sneaking around Merrick's cabins. Won't they smell you or whatever?"

"Are you saying I stink?"

He got a sideways eye roll for that one.

He chuckled. "They will. But since I was there anyway,

talking to Merrick, they won't think much of it. At least not until little Brian rats me out."

Bitsy turned to face him. "You were at Merrick's? Why?"

"I went to square things up with him for the scuffle with his brother, Stan." Glancing in the rearview mirror, he watched as a green Buick he thought might be tailing them got off the exit. His shoulders relaxed as he turned his attention back to the road.

"But I thought you said we needed to get out of there first thing in the morning."

"That was the plan, but you kind of forced my hand. I wanted to get you out of there before I went back to Merrick's."

"I don't understand."

He glanced over at her. "What did you think I was going to do? Just run away and hope Merrick didn't come after me for beating up his kid brother?"

"Well, sort of. Yeah."

He suddenly felt tired. All the time they'd spent together the last couple of days, and that's what she thought of him? "That's not the way it works, ittybit. Not for me. I don't run away from my responsibilities."

"Except when it involves standing up to your own pack."

He couldn't argue that point, and frankly, he was getting fucking tired of trying. So he said nothing.

After a while, she leaned her head back against the seat and fell asleep.

When they were nearly halfway home, he pulled off at a rest stop for gas. While it pumped, he got back in the cab and texted Stone to give him an update and let him know they were on their way back.

"Where are we?" Bitsy's voice was rusty with sleep as she squinted into the afternoon light.

"Amarillo or thereabouts. I just stopped for some gas."

She opened the door and hopped out.

"Where are you going?"

"To use the bathroom. And to get some shoes."

Before he could say another word, she slammed the door shut and darted between cars, heading toward the truck stop. Her quilted pants and T-shirt did nothing to hide her lush curves, and more than one male turned to watch her as she strutted across the lot in her bare feet.

Keegan topped off the gas tank and grabbed his keys out of the ignition, locking up the truck before following her inside. The gas pumps were on the opposite side of the lot to make room for the eighteen-wheelers, and by the time he got in there, she was flopping around in the ugliest pair of damn shoes in the store. With a wide grin, she skipped to the counter and handed over some cash to the clerk. Cash she must've stolen from his bag.

They were bright orange, plastic slip-ons with big white and purple flowers attached to the top. At least the purple matched her shirt, and her pants hid the cuff around her right ankle.

"Look!" She turned her grin on him when he appeared beside her, then looked down at her feet. "And they were only five dollars!"

She looked so happy by her find, he hated to burst her bubble. Still, he just couldn't see himself looking at those god-awful things all the way back to Austin. "You sure those are the shoes you want?" He glanced at the rack she'd found them on. "There are others here that are a little less…uh…"

"Happy?" She gave him a blinding smile with only the slightest tinge of sarcasm.

"Obnoxious," he corrected.

"Thank you," she told the clerk sweetly before walking past Keegan and out the door.

He paid for the soda he'd grabbed when he came in and with a shake of his head, followed her from the store. Her shoes were so distracting, even from the back, he almost didn't notice the guy with stringy hair and a beer gut walking away from the truck. When he saw them coming, he hustled into a black car parked at the pump behind them. The driver didn't even give him time to pull the door shut before it pulled out from behind the truck and left the parking lot with a squeal of tires.

Keegan frowned. Something wasn't right with what he'd just seen.

"You love these shoes," Bitsy called over her shoulder, drawing his attention back to her.

Something was wrong. And she was too far ahead of him.

"Bitsy, wait for me. Bitsy!"

The next few seconds happened all at once and yet so slowly it could've taken hours.

Bitsy stopped and half-turned to face him, her face screwed up at his bossy tone. Behind her, something sparked beneath his truck and the smell of burning wires carried across the lot to his sensitive nose.

Keegan broke into a run, shouting a warning.

Bitsy's eyes widened as she turned to see what he was pointing at.

His hat flew from his head as he hurled himself forward just as the truck exploded behind her.

The force of the blast lifted her off her feet and threw her backward.

Keegan adjusted at the last second and she hit him hard, her slight weight ramming into him with such force it knocked the air from his lungs. He hit the pavement with Bitsy on top of him. Her head smashed into his mouth, and Keegan tasted blood. He didn't know if it was hers or his. The skin on his back burned where he'd slid along the pavement.

Wrapping his arms around her, he rolled, tucking her beneath him as the gas pumps blew next.

Keegan lifted his head to a scene straight out of hell. A woman screamed over and over and ran for the cover of the store, dragging a small child behind her. Someone was on fire near the blast site. He couldn't tell if it was a man or a woman. They lurched around the parking lot like a drunken puppet, pulled by strings of orange flames. The acrid scent of burning flesh filled his nostrils.

As the shock started to wear off, it was replaced by a fury so intense everything went red. He couldn't breathe. He couldn't see.

Someone had just tried to take him out, and his heart with him.

Bitsy stirred beneath him, lifting her head. Slivers of glass glinted in her dark hair, and when she turned to look at the burning man—or woman—Keegan saw the singed strands around her face.

The anger threatened to consume him, and he took deep breaths through his nose and out his mouth as he watched the human fall to their knees and finally hit the pavement as the flames consumed them. The fact that it could easily have been Bitsy didn't escape him.

If she'd been only a few steps closer to the truck. If she hadn't stopped to look back at him while she teased him about her shoes—

The ground rumbled beneath him. He needed to move. They both needed to move. Pulling his legs and arms beneath him, Keegan got to his hands and knees. His body fought him every step of the way. His wolf pushed at its boundaries. It wanted to react to this threat, wanted to fight and protect. His muscles shifted, sliding around on his bones, and his skin felt hot and tight.

He reached for Bitsy, slid an arm under her chest to lift her from the ground and onto her feet, bringing her with him as he rose. She found her feet and turned, her hands gripping the front of his shirt as she looked around, her eyes dazed.

Her face was burned, the side that was facing the explosion bright red from the heat of the blast. Blisters covered her lower cheek and jaw. Her eye was swollen nearly shut from the burns.

Pain wracked through him as took in her injuries. The sight was too much. His wolf demanded retaliation.

Bitsy shouted at him, her fists pounding on his chest, then reaching for his face, pulling it down to hers, but he couldn't understand what she was saying.

Something else blew behind him, the noise so loud it shook the ground. Keegan bent forward, hiding his face in

Bitsy's neck, hiding from the humans as a fire truck came roaring onto the scene, sirens wailing. Bones cracked, muscles tore, and he wrapped his arms around her waist as his legs gave way, hunched in on himself, trying to hide what was happening.

Then suddenly they were moving. He closed his eyes against the smoke and grit his teeth against the agony of his broken body. A door slammed. When he opened them again, he could breathe easier and Bitsy was leaning against the closed door of the restroom.

"You're shifting."

"Way to point out the obvious." His voice was almost unrecognizable. Keegan grunted, absorbing the pain as his body contorted in ways that shouldn't be possible. The rest of the change was fast, but no less agonizing. When he was finished, he stood on four paws in the center of the room, head down, panting heavily.

He didn't know how she'd managed to get him in here in the condition she was in, but he was glad she had. Hopefully, with all the smoke and commotion, no one had noticed.

Her hands gripped the fur on each side of his jaw, lifting his face to hers. "Stay here, I'll be right back." And then she was out the door and gone.

Keegan rushed the door, but his teeth kept slipping on the knob, so he paced back and forth in the small room, his eyes never leaving the doorknob. Where the hell had she gone?

This was not helping him calm down.

And then she was back with an armful of clothes. "Okay. I think we're good. I don't think anyone noticed us, what with the flaming human and all." She fumbled with the lock on the knob, then pressed her back to the door and stared at him. She swayed, and slid down the door, landing hard on the floor. Looking around, her brows lifted in surprise. "This bathroom is surprisingly clean."

Keegan growled low in his throat as footsteps ran past outside.

"It's okay," Bitsy told him. "It's okay. We're good."

He didn't know if she was trying to convince him or herself.

"But, um, if you could change back now? That would be awesome." There were tears in her voice she was trying desperately to hide.

Shaking off the feeling of panic, Keegan stopped pacing and went to her. Bitsy's fingers tangled in his scruff, and he concentrated on the feel of them, on the fact that she needed him now. With that cuff around her ankle, she couldn't heal, not like she normally would. He needed to check her burns, then he needed to get them the hell out of here.

His emotions, heightened from all the commotion still happening outside the door, were hard to wrestle down, but eventually he managed. Bitsy's eyes never strayed from him as he shifted back, but there was nowhere he could hide, even if he'd wanted to.

When he was back to his human form, she held out the pile of clothes. "I think these will fit."

Covering his nakedness was the very last thing he was worried about right now, but she was right. He'd be much less conspicuous this way. He took the clothes from her. "Thank you."

She kept her face turned away while he slipped into the cheap sweats and the "I Like Big Trucks and I Cannot Lie" T-shirt.

"We need to get out of here," he told her. "But first, let me look at your face."

For once, she didn't argue as he knelt beside her and gently turned her head so he could see her burns.

"They don't look too bad." A lie. They looked horrendous and painful. But somehow, he knew making a big deal about it would only shut her down. "Is it only your face?"

Her brows lowered, and she winced when the movement hurt her. "I don't know."

"Will you let me look?"

After a brief pause, she nodded.

Keegan held her hand as she leaned forward so he could lift the back of her singed shirt. The skin along the right side of her ribcage was red and angry looking, but there were no blisters.

"I hate to tell you this, ittybit. But as soon as the shock wears off, you're gonna be in a world of hurt."

"Yeah, I kind of figured."

"Okay, let's go." Looping her left arm over his shoulders, he helped her to her feet. Pressing one ear to the door, he listened, but it was impossible to tell if anyone was right outside with all of the commotion. He sucked in a deep breath, opened the door, and took them both out into the open.

There were three fire trucks on the scene now. Firemen rushed around, shouting orders and hauling hoses as they tried to contain the blaze. Luckily, the store was far enough away that it only had minor damage from the explosion. Bystanders stood along the road, watching in fascinated horror as the burned body was loaded into an ambulance.

Keegan hustled around to the back of the building with Bitsy in tow. All he needed right now was for some well-meaning human to see them and try to "help." A four-foot wall bordered the back of the property, and on the other side of that wall was a new neighborhood. After another quick look to make sure no one was paying them any mind, Keegan boosted Bitsy up and over. He joined her and lifted her into his arms, being careful of her tender back. Then he started looking for an unoccupied home where they could hole up and use a phone, as he'd left his in the truck.

One looked promising a few houses down to the left. It was a smaller house, only one story, and of the same nondescript color the rest of them were. The yard was mostly dirt and there were no cars in the drive. The place looked abandoned. He ducked low along the fence and made his way to the house. As he cut across the yard, he cursed under his breath when he stepped on a bur.

"Bet you're wishing you had some happy shoes right about now," Bitsy said.

He would never admit it, but she had a point.

Keegan propped Bitsy up against the house and tried the back door. It was locked. Scrubbing the window clean with his sleeve, he peeked inside, looking for signs of an alarm system. When he didn't see a control panel anywhere, he took off his shirt, wrapped it around his fist, and smashed the decorative glass. Squeezing his arm through the opening, he unlocked the door and assisted Bitsy inside.

After he shook the glass out of his shirt, he put it back on and did a quick sweep of the place. The house was small and quaint, with a surprisingly large kitchen, two bedrooms and two baths, and a small fireplace in the living room. It also looked like it was brand new, or maybe between owners. Every room was freshly painted that light beige color common to the area, but there was no furniture, no personal items. Only bare floors and countertops, all wiped clean.

There was, however, a toolbox in the garage. Perhaps

left by a handyman who was doing some work on the place. Inside, Keegan found what he needed to get the iron cuff off Bitsy's ankle.

When he got back to the kitchen, she was sitting on the floor tiles, shivering.

Keegan made quick work of the cuff and chucked it out the back door. He even managed to get it off without injuring her further. Dried blood coated her torn skin from her efforts to escape, and he tried to wipe it off with a clean rag he'd found in the toolbox. When that didn't work, he tried the faucet, and was surprised to find both hot and cold running water.

He wet the rag with warm water, cleaned her ankle, and wet it again with cool water. This time, he placed it over the burns on her face.

She hadn't uttered a sound while he messed with her foot, but now Bitsy hissed in pain.

"I'm sorry," he told her sincerely.

Her eyes, one still swollen, shot to his face.

"I'm sorry," he told her again, and he realized he wasn't talking about her burns anymore. His vision blurred, and he blinked hard a few times. "I'm so sorry, Bitsy. I have no excuse for what I did. For what I allowed to happen. And I can't expect you to ever forget what I allowed to happen to you and your family."

She tugged on his arm until he removed the rag from her face. He was glad to see she was already healing, though he could tell there were still lingering effects from the iron. It would take a while for the effects to wear off completely.

"I'll never forgive you, Keegan." The words were

spoken softly and without malice, but they rang with honesty. "I can't."

Ah. The female knew how to gut him wide open better than anyone he'd ever known. She truly did. He brushed the uninjured side of her face with the back of his knuckles. Her skin was soft and supple, with only a light scattering of freckles to mar the perfection. No, "mar" was the wrong word. Her freckles were perfect. Perfect on her. A little bit of innocence complimented by the seductive tilt of her dark eyes and her perfectly kissable mouth.

Those lips were slightly parted, and she wet them with the tip of her tongue.

Keegan leaned in, his heart pounding in his chest, his blood roaring through his veins. He didn't know what he was thinking. She was hurt, in pain. But he just needed a taste. Just a little taste....

He saw her move a half second before her arm came up between them and her elbow slammed into his face. Bright spots of light floated in the air everywhere he looked and he tasted blood. "Dammit, Bitsy! What in the hell did you do that for?"

She took the wet rag from him and calmly lifted it to her face. "It looked like you were about to do something stupid, so I felt the need to stop you."

"Kissing you ain't stupid. It's probably the smartest thing I've ever done."

"And yet it won't be happening again."

"No?"

"No."

He rubbed his jaw. "We'll see about that."

She narrowed her eyes at him. "What's that supposed to mean?"

He didn't know why he was arguing with her. She was right. It shouldn't ever happen again. She was under his skin, affecting his decisions, his mood, everything. And had been since the first time he'd seen her.

It was like some sort of spell. The same sort of spell his father had been under.

No, that wasn't right. Keegan may be protective of the female in front of him, but his decisions still made sense. He still cared about his pack. His attraction to her was perfectly healthy and normal, not some type of bewitchment.

Shaking off thoughts of his father, he gave her a wink and got to his feet. "How's your back doing?"

"It feels hot."

"There's water. Do you feel like a lukewarm bath? It might soothe those burns until they have a chance to heal."

Her brow scrunched up with her typical irritability, but then her frown smoothed away. "Actually, that sounds pretty damn good."

He quickly suppressed the urge to grin like an idiot. But he couldn't help the surge of satisfaction that she was allowing him to care for her. Baby steps. "Do you think you'll be okay here by yourself if I run back over to the store and get us a few more essentials before the commotion dies down?"

"Mister play by the rules is gonna commit a crime?"

She obviously knew nothing about him. "I'm already wearing stolen clothes. Yours are half burned away, and we gotta eat." He didn't like the idea of leaving her there, but having her with him would only bring more attention their way. "If you don't wanna stay here alone—"

"I'll be fine," she told him. "Go."

Keegan paused before he went out the door. "If you hear anyone come in, just go out this door and wait for me by the wall."

"Just go," she said. "I'm fucking starving."

With one last look, he closed the door behind him and hauled himself up and over the wall. Either the people who lived in the neighborhood were all at work, or the chaos that was happening over at the gas station wasn't an unusual occurrence in this part of town, for there wasn't a curious soul to be seen.

He managed to make it into the store without anyone noticing. The employee who'd been working when it all went down was busy being interviewed by the police as the firemen worked to contain the fire. Keegan searched for his truck, and when he saw what little was left of it, he exhaled with relief. They'd never be able to track it to him.

Keegan moved fast. Too fast for the cameras to track him. Before he walked out, he put his purchases in bags he snagged from the counter so as not to attract any unwanted attention, and he even managed to grab some shoes that were only slightly small, though they weren't near as interesting as Bitsy's; just some slip-on sneakers.

When he got back to the house, Bitsy was exactly where he'd left her. He bent down in front of her and pulled the cloth from her face to check on things. The blisters and swelling were nearly gone, and only some slight redness remained. "It's looking good. How are you feeling?"

"Better." She eyed up the bags on the floor beside him. "What did you get?"

Keegan pulled out a to-go box and opened it. Inside, nachos were covered in melted cheese and piled high with tomatoes, sour cream, and jalapenos. No meat.

Her eyes lit up. "Holy shit. I think I love you."

An awkward silence followed her delighted exclamation, and it took a moment for Keegan to breathe again.

"Uh...I didn't mean...I just—"

"I also brought you this." He whipped out a bottle of iced tea and a variety of chocolate bars. "I wasn't sure what kind you like."

After a moment of indecision, Bitsy reached for the closest bar. "I like them all." She paused with a nacho halfway to her mouth. "Thank you, Keegan."

"Don't mention it." He sat down across from her and crossed his legs in front of him. "We gotta eat."

They passed the next half hour in silence. A few times, Keegan got caught staring at her, and she would look away self-consciously. He couldn't help it. It was damn near impossible to keep his eyes from her.

And she was softening toward him. She just wasn't ready to admit it.

When they were done, he showed her where the bathroom was and gave her some privacy, his only demand that she leave the door unlocked, just in case. Bitsy agreed without any argument. And honestly, it kinda worried him.

While he waited for her, he took a quick shower in the

other bathroom, glad he'd remembered to grab a few beach towels. When he was done, he knocked softly on Bitsy's door. "How you doin' in there, ittybit?"

No answer.

He knocked again, louder this time. Still no answer.

Keegan paced up and down the hall a few times. It was possible she was ignoring him, though he didn't see how it was likely. She'd been relatively compliant since they'd gotten to the house.

Maybe it was only the burns making her docile, and as they healed, her natural obstinacy was returning.

Keegan knocked again, and when she still didn't answer, he cracked the door and looked in on her.

Bitsy lay on her side in the tub with her face turned into the water so her burns were submerged. Only the side of her head and the curve of her hip were visible above the edge of the tub. Her arm covered her breasts, and her eyes were closed.

"Bitsy?"

She didn't move.

Well, she could be pissed at him all she wanted, but he was going to check on her. Keegan approached the tub, his only thought being to make sure she was okay. Yet that didn't stop his eyes from sweeping over her nude form, slightly distorted from the water. At the sight of all that smooth skin, his body hardened swift and fierce, and he had to stop for a moment and close his eyes, fists clenched at his sides so as not to touch her.

When he opened them again, he had himself somewhat under control. To keep things where they were at, he focused on her face. Her nose, with its dusting of freckles, was barely above the water. Keegan brushed her wet hair back from her forehead. Her skin was ice cold.

"Bitsy, wake up. You need to get out of this tub." When she didn't respond to his voice or his touch, he panicked. Heart racing, he reached into the water and sat her up, shaking her slightly. "Bitsy! Godammit! Wake up!"

Her eyes fluttered open, and Keegan nearly passed out as the blood caught up to his heart and pounded through his head. Grabbing the towel from the floor, he hauled her out of the water and set her on her feet in front of him before he wrapped it tight around her.

"What's wrong?" She scowled as she squinted at the truck on his T-shirt. "What are you doing?"

Keegan sat on the edge of the tub and pulled her onto his lap, tucking her head beneath his chin as he tried to warm her up. "You scared the ever-livin' hell out of me, Bitsy. You're ice fucking cold, and you wouldn't wake up."

She mumbled something into his shirt.

Though he didn't want to, he loosened his grip on her. "What?"

She repeated her words. "I must've just fallen asleep. The water felt good on my burns and my belly was full."

He took her chin and turned her face so he could check things out for himself. The redness was all but gone, the burns almost completely healed. Without thinking, he tugged at her towel to check her side.

"Hey!" She stood up, and the towel, gripped tight in Keegan's hand as he tried to keep her on his lap, was yanked from her hands and fell to the floor. Bitsy froze and stared at him, wide-eyed. But she didn't try to cover herself.

His breath froze in his lungs as his eyes ran from her bare feet, up her shapely calves and full thighs, to stop for a moment at the dark curls covering her pussy. They continued their journey over the rounded softness of her belly, to her full breasts tipped with large, dusky nipples. A light dusting of freckles were scattered above her areolas, and faded away as they reached her collarbone and neck.

Keegan reached for her and gripped her around her ribcage, just under the soft swells of her breasts, and tugged until she stepped toward him.

"Keegan—" Though she protested, there was no heat behind it.

"I just want to taste you." He tore his eyes from her nipples to glance up at her face.

There was a moment of indecision in her dark eyes before her fingers threaded through his hair to tighten in the curls at the nape of his neck. Her beautiful breasts rose and fell with her quick breaths, teasing him with their nearness, and the scent of her desire rose around him, blending with the fragrance of moonflowers.

Keegan wanted to rip off his clothes and take her down to the floor. He wanted to bury himself inside her warmth until he didn't know where he ended and she began.

But he did none of that. Because the desire to savor every second of this gift she was giving him overrode everything else.

Slowly, he pulled her closer. His mouth watered as he watched her nipples harden, the hard points straining toward him. He leaned in slowly, giving her time to change her mind, and flicked one gently with his tongue. Her skin was so soft and getting warmer by the second. Dropping soft kisses on the soft mounds, he made his way to the other one, and teased the tip with his tongue until Bitsy was arching her back, pushing against his hands to get closer.

She moaned in protest when he pulled away instead, her fingers tangling in his hair.

Lowering his head again, Keegan pressed kisses to each freckle, beginning on one side and working his way over to the other. He listened to the sounds she made, waiting for her to lose her patience, then he sucked a nipple into his mouth.

Bitsy hissed and dropped her head back, thrusting her breasts forward. Her legs moved restlessly between his, her knee brushing his hard cock, and Keegan bit her gently in warning.

Her hands were tugging at his shirt, and he released her nipple with his own groan of protest, so she could pull it up and off. Wrapping his arms around her hips, he pulled her close and pressed wet kisses to her stomach, under the curve of her breast, and back to her nipples. Her bare skin burned his everywhere she touched, and she was touching him everywhere she could as he suckled her.

Sliding his hands down to her rounded ass, he slid his fingers between her legs from behind, lifting her and spreading them wide to sit her back on his lap. The heat of her core scalded him through the thin material of his sweats, and Bitsy rocked her hips, stroking him with her body until he thought he would come in his pants.

When he could take no more, he stood, taking her with

him. She wrapped her legs and arms around him as he buried his face in her throat and pushed his pants down with one hand until his cock sprang free.

One arm wrapped around her waist, he held himself with the other, searching for her wet heat. With one hard thrust, he buried himself fully inside her, and his eyes rolled back in his head as his entire body shuddered.

Bitsy cried out as he claimed her. For that's exactly what this was, a claiming. Thoughts tried to creep into her head to ruin what was happening. Thoughts about who he was and what he had done. But then he lifted her away, and the raw agony of his loss had her tightening her legs around his waist until he was a part of her again.

He held her still as he shuffled around, and then she was being lowered onto the thick towel, spread out flat on the floor. As soon as she was all the way down she reached for him, opening her legs as he lowered himself between them. Pushing everything else away except the feel of him on top of her, Bitsy lifted her hips to meet him, her body straining upward like she was trying to reconnect with a part of herself that had been torn away, and she'd never realized it until this very moment.

Yet, still, something held her back from giving herself

to him completely. She kept her face turned away, avoiding the intimacy of his kisses, and kept her eyes squeezed tightly shut, avoiding his heated gaze that could see right into her soul. For as much as her body welcomed him, and her heart longed for him, she could not forgive him.

Keegan growled deep in his throat and renewed his efforts, as though the wolf inside sensed her rejection and was determined to overcome it. Bitsy moaned as he pulled out and cool air swept over her breasts and stomach. Her hips were lifted from the floor, and then his mouth was on her, his tongue relentless, working her up like he'd done it countless times before. The ache in her womb grew stronger, heavier, building in waves, until there was nothing but Keegan and the feel of his mouth and hands and what he was doing to her.

The wave rose, higher and higher. He held her tight as it crested, and Bitsy couldn't stop the words as she begged him to take her over the edge. With tongue and teeth and fingers, he did, drawing it out while her body jerked and shuddered beneath him until she thought she'd never breathe again.

She was still riding that wave of pleasure when he rose above her and slid inside, the thick length of him touching her womb. He drove in and out as Bitsy moaned beneath him, helpless to the pleasure that was building once again.

"Look at me," he ordered. His voice was tightly controlled.

But Bitsy just shook her head as a tear slid from the corner of her eye.

With a sound of frustration, he gathered her to him

and increased his thrusts until his roar joined her cries and she felt him come inside her.

Bitsy held him tight, not wanting to give up this moment. Not wanting reality to come crashing back.

"Bitsy—"

"Don't," she cut him off. "Just don't. Don't say anything. Please."

He sighed and dropped a kiss on her temple before he rolled away. But he didn't let go. Instead, he pulled her with him and tucked her against his side, holding her tight.

They lay like that for a long time, even though she knew the floor must be cold and hard beneath his back. But she didn't want to go back to reality. Not yet.

"Are you hungry?" he finally asked. "There's more food out in the kitchen. Then, once you're ready, we can go find a phone and call for a ride back to Austin."

Bitsy sighed as reality slammed into her bubble of contentment anyway. "I kind of am."

Before he left her alone to get dressed, he dropped a kiss on her nose. Bitsy closed her eyes, and he sighed.

When he was gone, she cleaned herself up and put on the clean clothes he'd brought her, similar to what he was wearing.

A picnic of sorts was waiting for her when she came into the kitchen. Keegan was sitting cross-legged on the floor. In front of him was an array of sandwiches, chips, and more bottles of tea.

He got to his feet when she appeared in the doorway. "I hope egg salad is okay."

Bitsy ran her eyes over him. Even in sweats, a silly T-shirt, and old-man shoes, he was still an imposing figure.

And hot. *So* fucking hot.

She sat down, and he joined her. "Egg salad is good. Thank you."

"You look good," he told her. "Your burns, I mean. They're gone."

She nodded and took a bite of her sandwich. It was pretty good for gas station food.

"Bitsy—"

Mid-chew, she held up her hand, cutting him off. "Don't." She didn't know what he was about to say, but by the tone of his voice, it was bound to be an apology of some sort. And she was so fucking tired of his apologies.

Keegan dropped his sandwich on the wrapper. "No. You need to hear this, dammit. And I need to say it."

She swallowed the bite she was chewing and started gathering up her trash. Bitsy didn't know why she was so averse to letting the guy talk, she just knew she didn't want to hear it. If he said it, it would ruin everything.

Or, somehow, he would talk her into forgiving him. And that was even scarier.

"I was wrong," he told her. "I was completely fucking wrong. And worse than that, I was a coward. I *am* a coward."

Bitsy stilled. He was waiting for her to look at him. She couldn't do it. She just couldn't. If she looked at him, she would see the sincerity in his face. She would see the honesty and self-loathing in his green eyes that she heard in his voice.

And she would forgive him for what he did to her. She would. All of the pain, all of the humility, would mean nothing if she could possess his heart.

He tilted her chin up, and Bitsy averted her eyes.

"Dammit, Bitsy. LOOK at me." He tightened his fingers on her jaw, sticking his face so close she had no choice. His eyes caught hers and wouldn't let go. His were bright and red with unshed tears. "I can never say this in front of the pack, can never admit to this weakness to anyone but you, but I was dead wrong, ittybit. The rodeo, the way I allowed them to treat you and your family, it's fucked up. It's all completely fucked up. You were treated like animals. And I loathe myself for it. I don't want your forgiveness. I just need you to hear me. To really *hear* me. I'm *sorry*."

She heard him. She heard him loud and clear. "Even animals don't deserve to be treated like that."

One corner of his mouth turned up in derisive smile, and his hand dropped back onto his lap. "You're right. They don't."

She studied his rugged face. "Why are you telling me this?"

"Don't you know?"

Bitsy did know. She just didn't want to admit it. "You can apologize to me all day and night, Keegan. It doesn't change what happened in the past."

"I know that. But I'm hoping maybe it will change what happens in the future."

"Between us, you mean."

He gave her a nod. "Yes. Between us."

"What if I told you there won't ever be an 'us'?"

"I refuse to believe that, ittybit."

"That's a mistake on your part."

"I don't think so. You want me as much as I want you. You just proved it."

She knew he would do that. She knew if she gave in to her body's needs he would throw it back in her face. "Maybe I just like sex, and you were the closest warm body around."

The smirk fell from his face. "You're lying." He pointed toward the bathroom. "That meant something to you. And it sure as hell meant something to me."

"It meant I was horny."

Keegan cocked his head and stared at her. Bitsy met his gaze unflinchingly.

Then he chuckled and started gathering up the remains of their dinner. "You just keep telling yourself that, ittybit." Stuffing everything in a bag, he stood and offered her a hand.

Bitsy ignored it and stood up without assistance.

"Get those obnoxious shoes on and we'll go find a phone."

That sounded great to her. She was ready to get the hell out of this house, and away from everything that had happened there. Bitsy knew she was running away—from Keegan, and from herself. From what she longed for. Because she could deny it all she wanted to him, but she couldn't lie to herself.

She wanted Keegan. And she always had. It was the way the gods had decided to bring them together she had an issue with.

"Oh, wait." She'd nearly forgotten. "I have a phone. It's in my pants pocket."

"Did it survive the explosion?"

She was already heading down the hall. "We'll see." When she got to the bathroom, she found the phone. It was alive and kicking. Gathering up the rest of her clothes, she took it out to Keegan.

In no short order, he made a call and they had a rental car heading their way. They left the house, deciding it would be better to wait at a nearby laundry mat just down the service road.

The rental car was there within thirty minutes, and they were on their way back to Austin.

"Who do you think did it?" she asked once they were back on the highway.

Keegan adjusted the rearview mirror, then shot her a sideways glance. "I don't know. I saw a guy walking away from the truck right before it blew. I didn't recognize him."

"You can't think of anyone who'd want to blow you up?"

"Not offhand, no."

Bitsy turned back to the window. Texas scenery hadn't improved overnight. Nothing but flat fields of straw-like grass, cactus, and the occasional sorry excuse for a tree to distract her from her thoughts. There was no color, either. Just various shades of brown.

"How is your mom?"

The question took her by surprise, and she stiffened. "My mom?"

"Yeah, your mom. And your cousin, Bronaugh, was it?"

He caught her staring at him as if he'd lost his mind. "What?"

"What do you care?"

"Bitsy, don't start this shit again."

"Seriously, Keegan. You're only asking because you're trying to win me over."

"That's not true."

"It is true. You fuck me once and suddenly think everything is normal between us? I've got a newsflash for you. It's not."

"Don't presume to know what I think, or how I feel."

His tone surprised her more than the words. "All right, then. How do you feel? Huh? Tell me, Keegan. Tell me how you feel." She nearly spit the words at him.

Keegan wrenched the wheel to the right and brought the car to a skidding halt on the side of the highway. Throwing it into park, he sat for a minute with his hands clenched so tight on the wheel his knuckles were white. He released it only to slam his palms against it in a burst of anger. Then he placed them on his thighs and leaned his head back against the headrest, taking deep breaths.

Bitsy drew back, surprised by his burst of emotion. She was being a bitch, and she knew it. But he deserved some bitchiness from her, and more. "You told me…"

Before she could finish the sentence, her seatbelt was unclipped, and she was plucked from her seat and onto his lap. Her pulse pounded as he took her face between his palms so she couldn't look away or get off his lap.

"You wanna know how I feel, ittybit? I feel like kissing that sassy mouth of yours until the only word coming from it is my name. And then I feel like tearing these ridiculous clothes from you until your bare skin is hot on mine. And then I feel like tasting your luscious pussy on my tongue until you're shaking with the need to come. After that, I feel like sinking into your tight little body until *I'm* shaking with the need to come. And I feel like doing all that right here in front of all of Texas."

His eyes glowed brighter than any fire, burning the truth of everything he'd just said right into her soul. And with every word, he hardened beneath her ass. Even the muscles in his chest seemed to grow beneath her palms until his maleness filled the small space and there was nothing but him.

His green eyes boring into hers, his smell—like the outdoors and the clean scent of soap—the warmth of his body, the roughness of his palms on her cheeks.

"That's not what I meant," she managed to rasp.

With a low growl, he pulled her face to his and took her mouth. His kiss wasn't gentle, and in it she felt all his frustration, all his regret, and all his need. Bitsy's hands curled into fists on his shoulders, gripping the thin cotton of his T-shirt in an effort not to expose her own need.

But it wasn't necessary, for he ended the kiss with a sharp bite to her lower lip and plopped her back in her seat, leaving her head swimming and her blood roaring through her veins. Her clothes were too heavy on her sensitized skin, and she was wet between her legs.

"When we get back to Austin, I'm coming up to your room. And I'm not leaving until you're either out of my system or you've accepted me as yours." With that statement, Keegan threw the car into drive and accelerated onto the highway, cutting off oncoming cars and sending them veering out of the way with angry honks.

"Okay," Bitsy whispered. With shaking hands that had nothing to do with fear and everything to do with how much she wanted the male sitting in the driver's seat, she refastened her seat belt.

CHAPTER 15

It took every ounce of self-control Keegan had not to take Bitsy right there on the side of the highway in broad daylight with half of Texas flying past them. It would've been easy. They were both only wearing sweat pants and T-shirts from the gas station, as the clothing options available there had been limited.

But a quick fuck wasn't what he wanted. Not with her. With Bitsy, he wanted nights full of soft sighs and hot whispers and her little, curvy body tangled up with his. He wanted early mornings with coffee on the porch as they listened to the birds and talked about the past and their hopes for the future and watched the sun come up. He wanted to argue with her. He wanted to laugh with her. He wanted stolen kisses and quick romps on the kitchen counter and long, slow explorations of every inch of her lush body in front of the fire on a rainy day. He wanted it all. He always had. He'd just been waiting for her.

He shook those thoughts from his head and concentrated on the road. At least he'd managed to shut her sweet mouth. For the time being, anyway.

The seven-hour drive back to Austin took him five in the high-end vehicle he'd managed to secure for them.

It was the longest five hours of his life.

Occasionally, Bitsy would squirm around restlessly on the seat beside him. He thought about reaching over there a few times to help her ease her discomfort, but he didn't. He wanted her uncomfortable. He wanted her to think of nothing but him and how he made her feel. He wanted her to crave him as he craved her.

Even if he didn't deserve it, and even if he risked going down like his old man.

After what was the longest road trip in history, he pulled up in front of the hotel. A shiver ran down his spine as he got out of the rental and let the valet take it, but ghosts be damned. He was going up to that room come hell or high water.

Bitsy glanced at him nervously as she preceded him inside, and he half expected her to object his company, but she didn't.

They were halfway across the lobby when Keegan heard Stone's heavy drawl.

"It's about time y'all got back."

Bitsy froze in front of him, her spine ramrod straight. She recognized the voice, too.

Keegan turned to see his second rising from the old-fashioned armchair he'd been lounging in and come strutting toward them. When he arrived, he shook hands with Keegan and gave Bitsy a smile Keegan couldn't quite read. "Y'all know this place is haunted, right?"

Bitsy shot Stone a look that would have a normal man withering at her feet, then she turned her back on him and said to Keegan, "I'm going upstairs."

"You'll need a new room key," he reminded her.

"Right." Turning on her heel, she marched over to the front desk in her god-awful shoes.

Keegan watched her walk away, wondering if she'd get him one this time, and then turned back to find Stone staring at him with open curiosity and a touch of *you've got to be kidding me.*

"What's going on with that one, Keegan?"

"None of your fucking business."

Stone held both hands up in front of him, palms out. "All right, man. All right. Just asking." Shoving his hands in his pockets, his grin widened. "What's going on with these clothes, then?"

"Long story. What the hell are you doing here, Stone? Why aren't you at the ranch?"

"I had to leave the ranch. I've been waiting here—"

Keegan slashed through the air with his hand to cut him off. "*Had* to leave? What happened?"

Stone touched his hat as Bitsy walked past with her new room key.

She ignored them both completely and headed straight for the grand stairway.

Stone lowered his voice. "Merrick showed up with his pack, just a few hours ago. They brought a few 'gifts' along with them."

"I don't understand. I just left Merrick. What gifts?"

Stone shook his head. "Ones like her." He pointed with his chin toward the staircase.

"What tribe?"

"How the hell can you tell? None of them are zombied out like the other two we had, but that don't mean nothin'. Maybe they just didn't turn yet."

Keegan put his hands on his hips and stared at the floor, thinking furiously. "What did he do with them?"

"He locked them up in the barn, then he proceeded to take over the house. I snuck on out of there shortly after to come warn you."

The barn was where they held their rodeos, and where the iron cells were where Bitsy and her family had been held.

"Won't he notice you're gone?"

"Of course he will. But he didn't try to stop me."

"Which means he'll be waiting for me when I get back."

Stone nodded. "Oh, one more thing."

Keegan lifted one eyebrow in question.

"He was asking for her."

"Merrick?"

"No, man. The Faerie dude. Well, he asked for another one first, and said she would've been with that one." Again, he indicated the stairs Bitsy just walked up. "Or, so I assume. He described her to a 'T'."

Keegan clenched his fists and ground his teeth together to keep himself from knocking the look off of Stone's face. "Her *name* is Bitsy."

Stone stilled when he noticed his Alpha's posturing. "Sure, man. Sorry. He was looking for *Bitsy*."

Keegan looked away, not quite believing he was on the verge of knocking out one of his best friends in the middle of the hotel lobby. He needed to get a grip. "Is he an older man?"

"I think so. But again, it's hard to tell with them."

"Son of a bitch." He thought hard. "Okay. Go back to the ranch, but don't let yourself be seen. However, do NOT let anyone near that male. Do whatever you have to do. He's to be treated with southern fucking hospitality until I can get there and take care of this situation with Merrick. Is that understood?"

"Sure thing, man."

"And be careful, Stone. Do not let Merrick or any of his pack catch your sorry hide sneaking around there."

"Got it." He started to turn away. "Are you coming?"

Keegan glanced toward the stairway. "I'll be along within the hour. I need to deal with something first."

"Keegan, can I just say—"

"No."

"But, look. As a friend—"

Keegan released the Alpha until his voice vibrated with it. "I said no."

Stone lowered his head and backed away, but Keegan didn't miss the look of disapproval on his face. "I'll see you at home." Then he turned on his boot heel and strode from the hotel.

Keegan took a deep breath. He had no doubt in his mind the Fae currently being held in his barn was Bitsy's father. She was right. He had been in Colorado. As a "guest" of Merrick's. It had all been part of his plan to get Keegan away from the ranch for a few days.

But why now? What was he after?

Taking the stairs two at a time, he went to Bitsy's

room. He still hadn't decided what he was going to tell her by the time he knocked on her door. He wasn't sure he wanted to tell her anything at all. At least, not until they'd finished what they'd started in the car.

But when the door opened and she stood staring up at him with those dark eyes, he knew he had to be straight up with her. The trust between them was tenuous at best right now. If he tried to lie or hide it from her, or put his needs before her own, it would ruin any strides he'd recently made.

"Hi," she said. "Is everything okay?"

"Can I come in?"

She stepped back and gave him room to enter, shutting and locking the door behind him. Then she leaned back against it. "What's happened?"

Keegan rubbed the back of his neck. "You know how you told me you 'felt' your father back in Colorado? And then it was gone?"

"Yes." She eyed him warily.

"I think I know where he went."

She shoved away from the door. "What? Where? Where is he?"

"Merrick is here. And he brought a group of Faeries with him. To the ranch."

Bitsy stilled. "The rodeo, you mean."

"The barn," he corrected. "Apparently, he showed up there today. Just a few hours ago. Stone said the male was asking for, I assume, your mother. And then he described you."

"What did they tell him?"

"Nothing that I know of."

"Did you tell him to take my father out of the cell?"

"No, I didn't."

"Why the fuck not?"

Keegan lifted his eyebrows at her tone. "Because leaving him there will ensure he stays in one place until I can get you to him. I sent Stone back to the ranch. I told him to stay out of sight, but he's keeping an eye on your dad. He'll make sure he's not harmed."

She stared at him, but he couldn't read her expression. "Just let me get changed."

A feeling of foreboding rose within him. He didn't like the idea of her going back to there. "I can go see him. You don't have to go back there, ittybit."

But she shook her head. "No. I want to go. I need to see for myself."

"See that I'm not lying to you? Is that it?"

Her silence was answer enough.

"Dammit, Bitsy." Keegan scrubbed his face with his hands and paced away from her. "I don't want you coming anywhere near the ranch. Not right now. Let me go alone, and I'll bring your father to you here." He didn't want to tell her what Merrick's presence could mean. Him showing up like this after Keegan took Bitsy from him could mean one of two things: he brought the others as a contribution to the rodeo and wanted no hard feelings between them, or his showing up uninvited, with his pack in tow, was a challenge to Keegan's authority.

He had a pretty strong feeling it was the latter.

Bitsy laid her hand on his chest.

Her touch instantly calmed the agitation and indecision within him, and he stilled beneath her small palm.

Her dark eyes lifted to his, and for the first time, the wall of defense he'd always sensed between them—the wall that was there even when he was inside of her—was gone. "I want to trust you, Keegan. I really do. Take me with you. If Merrick is up to something, I'll be safer with you than here by myself."

She may have a point. Merrick had correctly guessed his every move so far. He covered her hand on his chest with both of his. He couldn't refuse her. Not when she was looking at him that way. He cupped her cheek in his palm. "Go get changed, and then we'll go see your father."

Bitsy was silent for the entire trip out to the ranch. She'd changed back into a pair of shorts—purple and lacy —and a Stevie Nicks concert T-shirt. Her ugly orange shoes topped it off.

Her sense of style, or lack thereof, never ceased to amaze him.

When Keegan pulled off the main road and onto the dirt drive leading up to the house, she began to twist her hands in her lap.

"You can control your pack, right?" she asked.

Keegan took her hand to still her fidgeting. "Honestly, I don't know what's going on with anything right now. Stay with me everywhere I go. I won't leave you alone."

"Okay."

"I still don't like this, Bitsy."

She gave him a small smile. "I know."

He pulled up to the house.

"He's here," Bitsy told him breathlessly.

"You sure?"

She nodded. "Yes. I feel him."

Once he had Bitsy inside, he looked around for Merrick or any of his pack, but the house was unusually quiet. He assumed Bitsy would want to go straight to the barn, but instead, she stopped by the stairs. Reaching up, she gripped the railing in a white-knuckled grip.

"Ittybit, I can go get him and bring him outside."

"You promised not to leave me alone," she reminded him.

"That I did."

"I just need a minute."

Her face was too pale, and his chest ached to see her fear, and know that he was the one who caused it. "Let's take a minute, then. He ain't going anywhere, and I'd like to change out of these gas station clothes, too."

She nodded her agreement, and he took her upstairs to his room. With the turn of every corner, Keegan half expected Merrick or one of his boys to jump out, but the house appeared to be empty.

Once they arrived at his room, she stood at the window with her back to him as he swapped his sweats for jeans, boots, and a lightweight plaid shirt. He joined her at the window, looking out at the building where she'd been held and forced to participate in the rodeo just weeks before.

He unbuttoned his shirt cuffs and rolled up his sleeves. "You all right, ittybit?"

She turned from the view and took a deep breath. "What do you think?"

"I think that was a stupid question." Keegan approached her cautiously, half expecting her to bolt. But she held her ground, and his admiration for her grew in leaps and bounds. This was one extremely brave little female. Or extremely stubborn. But either way, it only made him want to protect her more. He brushed the back of his knuckles down her cheek. Her skin was so soft, so smooth, and he knew it was like that everywhere. "I can take you out of here. Take you back to the hotel. Take you to a different hotel. Just say the word, darlin'. And we're gone."

"And what about my father?"

"I'll come back and get him. Bring him to you."

But she shook her head. "He wouldn't believe you. He wouldn't come with you."

"Maybe you could give me something to give him. Let him know it's safe."

She took a deep breath. "No. I'm already here."

It was more than that. Keegan knew it was more. She was testing him. At the risk of her own safety.

And he would fucking pass this test with flying colors. No matter what it took. "All right. Let's go, then." He held out his hand, and this time, she took it, lacing her fingers through his and holding on tight.

CHAPTER 16

Bitsy followed Keegan down the stairs and out of the house. She had the fleeting impulse to run, but displaying any sign of weakness in front of a predator would only invite them to use that weakness.

It occurred to her she should have called Duncan, just to let them know where she was, but with everything that had happened, she just hadn't thought about it. For all the Seattle pack knew, Keegan had gone back on his word and was again using her for the entertainment of the wolves. But Duncan and Lucian were close by. They would come check on her as soon as enough time had passed and she still hadn't checked in.

Or they would assume everything was fine. It was a fifty-fifty chance.

Bitsy gave a shaky sigh, and Keegan glanced over his shoulder with a reassuring wink. At least, she assumed it was meant to be reassuring, but in reality, all it did was make her forget to breathe for a few seconds.

One step at a time. She just had to take it one step at a time. Already, she could feel her senses dulling as they approached the large barn looming before her, every board laced with veins of iron. It weakened her, cut off her connection with nature and its creatures.

But something else was growing stronger the closer she got.

It was her father.

Bitsy' heart sped up with excitement. Keegan had been right. Her father was here, a prisoner the same way she had been. And again, the male walking beside her, the one holding her hand so sweetly, had done nothing to stop it.

Yet, she couldn't bring herself to let go.

Until they got to the door.

Bitsy dug in her heels. "I can't go in there, Keegan."

He scanned the area, as did Bitsy. No curious eyes followed them. No one lurked around outside the house to watch what was going on.

"I can go in and get him and bring him out here to you."

Bitsy let go of his hand and realized hers was slick with sweat. She dried her palms on her shorts and gave him a jerky nod. "Okay. Thank you."

Keegan gave her a reassuring smile, his eyes searching her face as though he wanted to say something. But in the end, he just returned her nod. "Holler if you need me. I'll hear you."

She watched as the door closed behind him, and then she was alone. Much as she wanted to put some distance between herself and the barn, she didn't dare. She'd put her life in Keegan's hands by coming here, and strangely enough, she found she trusted him. So, she would stay where he could hear her if she needed help.

She tried to swallow around her dry throat.

Though she couldn't see anyone, Bitsy felt them watching her. There were eyes everywhere. Watching, waiting, surrounding her like wolves did when they were hunting prey. But none came near.

The back door to the house opened and a female stepped out. She was tall and willowy, with dark hair and eyes so light, Bitsy couldn't tell the color from this distance. Striding to the top of the stairs, the female crossed her arms and leaned against the post. Watching. Her casual pose doing nothing to hide the silent threat in her expression.

Corrina.

Bitsy knew this member of Keegan's pack quite well, and at one time was under the impression she was the Alpha's mate. She was a constant presence ringside during the rodeo events, and often guarded the only way out of the iron cage that enclosed the arena. Though she never took part, she would cheer on the others with a disgusting enthusiasm whenever the shifters got one up on the Fae who were unlucky enough to play the part of the livestock.

Bitsy felt a familiar surge of bile at the sight of her, but she refused to be cowed. Though she felt some effects, she was not chained and locked in a jail of iron now. Let the bitch try something, and she would show her exactly how scary the Fae could be.

The barn door opened behind her, and Bitsy spun around, a smile turning up the corners of her mouth. But the expression froze on her face when she saw it was only Keegan.

Something was wrong.

"Corrina!" he called upon spotting her on the back porch. "Where is the key?"

"Why? Do you need it to lock her up?" She looked pointedly at Bitsy.

"Where is my father, Keegan?"

"He's in there, along with some others that must have been with him."

"But you don't have the key."

"That would be correct, ittybit." He sighed heavily. "There's no guard and no key."

"No one else is in there who can let him out?"

His gaze was steady on hers. "No one else."

This was a direct act of defiance by his entire pack, a challenge to his position as pack master. And she had a good guess who was leading the charge. "Where is Merrick?"

"Hell if I know, but I'm about to find out."

"Wait." She grabbed his wrist as he walked past her. Her stomach twisted until she thought she was going to be sick at the thought of going in there, but she had to see for herself. "I need to see him. I need to see my dad."

The look on Keegan's face spoke volumes. "Of course. I wasn't thinking. Come on. I'll take you in." He shot Corrina a look over his shoulder, promising her this was not over, then opened the large barn door and held it for Bitsy.

Taking one last deep breath of fresh air, Bitsy ducked under his arm and went inside.

It still smelled the same, like sawdust and motor oil and sweat—and fear. They had to walk through the arena to get to the hallway between the bleachers that led to the back rooms where the cells were located. Bitsy glanced around nervously, but they appeared to be alone. "What are you going to do?"

"I'm going to take you to see your dad. And then I'm going to take you to a hotel and call Cedric to get you the hell out of here. And then I'm going to come back and deal with my pack."

"I'm not going anywhere without my father."

Keegan stopped, his hand on the door to the arena. "I can't have you here when this is going down, ittybit. I shouldn't have let you talk me into bringing you here." He glanced around. "All of this is downright unnerving. I don't know what, exactly, Merrick is up to. But I can tell you, it ain't good."

Bitsy felt the urge to reassure him. But he was right. Something was about to go down.

"I'll get your dad out and make sure he gets to Seattle. I swear it to you."

"What if you lose? How will you get him out then?

"Bitsy—"

"Your pack, or Merrick, is challenging your leadership. That's what's happening, right? I know how shifters work. You're going to have to fight to hold onto your position as Alpha. Fight to the death. So, what if you lose? What will happen to my father?" What would happen to her if she lost him before she ever had a chance to really have him?

He dipped his head, hiding his features beneath the brim of his hat, and Bitsy had her answer.

"It won't happen," he insisted. "But I can't take care of this with you around. You're too much of a distraction. I'd be so busy worrying about you, I wouldn't be able to do what I had to do. And if that happened, I can guarantee it won't just be your father back in that cell." He pointed toward the hall that led to the cell room.

Bitsy tried to suppress the feeling of panic rising in her throat. But surprisingly, it wasn't herself she was worried about. "If you lose, you'll be dead."

One side of Keegan's mouth lifted in something resembling a smile. "Careful there, darlin'. You almost sound like you care."

Now it was Bitsy's turn to look away so he wouldn't see how right he was. It wasn't the time or the place to get into an uncomfortable declaration of feelings. "Is there no way to get my father out first? So, he can come with me?"

"I don't know. But I can sure as hell try."

She swiped at her eyes where a suspicious moisture was gathering. "Okay. Let's do that, then."

He nodded and held the door open to the arena.

She took a deep breath and entered the arena. The door clanked shut behind them, and Bitsy jumped.

"It's all right, ittybit. Nothing's gonna happen to you in here."

"Not this time?" she asked with more than a trace of sarcasm.

"Not ever again," he said with such intensity, Bitsy almost believed him.

"I wouldn't be making promises I couldn't keep, Keegan."

The words came from behind them, the female voice snide.

Bitsy spun around as the door to the arena rattled and Corrina secured the lock.

Keegan strode over to the door. "Let us out, Corrina."

The timbre of the Alpha vibrated within his deep voice, and Bitsy could see how it affected the female shifter by the way she lowered her head and clenched her hands into tight fists.

But, somehow, Corrina managed to resist. She shook her head hard, backing away.

"Corrina!"

"I'm sorry, Keegan. But I can't let you do this."

"It's not your place to 'let' me do anything. I am your Alpha. Are you forgetting that? Open the goddamn door. Unless you want to come in here right now and challenge me for that position?"

Bitsy backed away, struggling to breathe as the tension grew thick. Shudders ran over Keegan's body in waves, and she watched as the skin on his forearms shifted on the muscle. He was losing his temper, and she didn't want to get caught in the middle if there was about to be a wolf fight.

"Cor's not the one you need to worry about, my friend. She's just a bitch. We both know she's not Alpha material. But she'll make me one hell of a mate."

Bitsy whipped around to see Merrick sprawled on one of the motorcycles lined up at the end of the arena, used in lieu of horses, because horses would spook as soon as a werewolf came anywhere near them.

He must've been inside the entire time. And now she

was super grateful things hadn't gotten personal between her and Keegan, because how fucking embarrassing. But how did he not know Merrick was there?

A horrible thought occurred to her. She tried to push it away, but it persisted, clanging around in her head like the lyrics of a bad disco song. Maybe she was being naïve. Maybe he'd known all this time. And maybe this was all some elaborate setup to get her back where he'd wanted her all along.

Petting the handlebars as he admired the detail on the grips, Merrick said, "This would've been so much easier if you'd had a chance to get in the truck before it blew."

Okay, so maybe Keegan *wasn't* in on this.

Keegan stilled, staring at Merrick as though he'd never seen him before. He sidestepped and placed himself between Merrick and Bitsy, and much as she hated to do it, she moved closer and allowed him to act as a shield. Encased by the iron bars of the cage that covered the arena, there was very little chance of fighting her way out of there.

She'd been stupid to come in here again.

She'd been stupid to come anywhere near this state again. And if she got out of this alive, she was getting the hell out of Texas and she wouldn't be coming back. Not for anything.

Keegan glanced at her over his shoulder before turning back to face the Colorado Alpha. His green eyes were apologetic and worried.

No, if she made it through this she wouldn't come back for anything.

Or anyone.

CHAPTER 17

Keegan cursed under his breath. He wasn't worried about his own safety. What would happen would happen. He'd accepted this fate the first time he'd been challenged for his new position of Alpha at sixteen. And if he were honest about it, not having the responsibility of being the Alpha would almost be a relief.

Except for the whole "fight to the death" part.

But he was worried about what would happen to Bitsy if he didn't win this fight. He shouldn't have brought her in here. He should've left her at the hotel, as he'd originally decided before she'd turned those big, brown eyes on him, and come back alone to deal with all of this. He should have never brought her here at all. He should've left her in Austin while he fetched her faather for her. And if he'd been unsuccessful, once she was safely with her mother, the Seattle pack would have helped her get her father back. He was sure of it. They were stand-up guys and considered her one of their own.

But no, he had to try to be her fucking hero. And now he might get them both killed.

Or worse.

He wondered where the hell Stone was. Was he really innocent in all of this? Or was he part of this whole elaborate plan and just too much of a chickenshit to show his face?

Merrick continued talking as he stroked the motorcycle like a lover. "See, my guy saw you both leave the store, and he panicked. He miscalculated the time it would take you to get close enough to the truck when it blew." He looked off into the distance, pushing his glasses up on his nose with his index finger. "I guess it was partly my fault. I was extremely explicit with my instructions. Let you both get right up on the truck, but don't give you time to toss the bomb." He smiled at Keegan. "I knew you would notice it. You're smart like that." He tapped the side of his head.

"What do you want, Merrick?" Keegan asked him. If he could just keep him talking, maybe he could figure out a way to get Bitsy out of there. He could already see the affects of the iron weakening her. She wouldn't have a chance against him and Corrina. "Where's the rest of my pack?"

"Corrina sent them away for the day on various errands."

Keegan turned his body just enough that he could look at Corrina.

She cowered under his icy gaze, but it gave him little gratification. "Because you know they would never allow this to happen," he told her.

"They won't have a choice," she said. "By the time they get back, the fight for Alpha will be over. They'll accept the winner."

No, they wouldn't. Not without witnesses. Keegan smiled. It didn't quite reach his eyes. "You'd better hope and pray that it ain't me, Cor. I don't take kindly to betrayal, to me, my girl, or my pack."

Corrina glanced over his shoulder at Merrick and lifted her chin.

And he saw the utter truth in that gesture. She wasn't affected by his threat. She didn't expect him to win.

Her defiance hit him like a branding iron right in the gut. Corrina had been with him for a long time, and though there'd never been anything romantic between them, they'd always been close. She was like a little sister to him. If Keegan had to guess who would be the one to betray him, out of all of the shifters in his pack, she would've been his last choice.

Seems he'd been nothing but a blind fool. He'd underestimated her loyalty.

"We're wasting time," Merrick said, a little louder than necessary.

Keegan shot one last look at Cor. It would be the last time. From here on out, she was dead to him.

A plan formed. He didn't think it would work, but he had to try. "Let Bitsy out of here. She doesn't need to be in the middle of this."

Merrick's gaze shifted to Bitsy.

Keegan didn't like the look in his eyes. He didn't like it at all.

"I don't think so. I've always...admired this one. She's

spunky. I've spent many nights pondering how to get you to give her up. At least until you decided to be a pussy and let her leave with the rest of your entertainment. But never fear! I came up with a plan to get her back."

"And her father was a part of that plan." It was all coming together now.

Merrick shrugged. "I didn't know he was her father at the time, only that he was a part of the group who had wandered off, and therefore, was missed when you caught her and her mother. Still, I had high hopes he would be of good use. But when she wandered right onto my land of her own free will and I finally had a chance to get to know her better, she was stolen from me. And you were the one who did the stealing. Fucking up my plans. AGAIN." His eyes dropped to Bitsy's breasts and hips and back to her face. "Still, I could've just let her go. But I think I'd like to keep her."

A predatory growl filled the cavernous space, vibrating the iron bars of the cage. It took Keegan a moment to realize it was coming from him, but there was no holding it inside. His entire body shook with rage.

But Merrick just lifted his eyebrows in question.

"She doesn't belong to you," Keegan told him.

"She doesn't belong to you, either. Not anymore. You let her go."

"He did. And I came back. But not for this shit."

Keegan was surprised to hear Bitsy speak up.

"I came back of my own free will. Because I don't 'belong' to anyone, asshole."

Merrick laughed. "Ah, yes. There's that fire I remember."

But her show of defiance didn't turn him off. If anything, Keegan saw by the gleam in his eyes that his interest in her only increased. Like him, Merrick appreciated a challenge. But unlike him, it was only because he was bored with his long life. Not because he appreciated a female who knew her own mind and was his equal in courage and a lust for life. He may have not expressed that lust correctly in the past, but it was something he was determined to correct.

If he had the chance.

"Why are you doing this, Merrick? You have your own pack to worry about. Why the sudden interest in mine?"

Merrick's eyes shifted from Bitsy to Corrina, and Keegan felt like someone had just taken off his blinders. It wasn't Bitsy Merrick wanted—at least not in the way Keegan thought. It was Corrina. And for the first time since he'd known her, he saw her cheeks flush self-consciously as she gazed up from under her lashes.

It appeared the affection wasn't one-sided. And that explained the sudden loyalty switch. Love didn't care whose side you should be on.

"Ah. I get it." Crossing his arms over his chest, he attempted to buy some time. "But I still don't get why the play for my pack? If you want Cor, and it's obvious she wants you"—the color rose even higher in her cheeks—"then why not go about mating with her the normal way and have her swear her loyalty to you? Why *try* to take my pack?" He purposely left Bitsy out of the conversation, wanting to draw Merrick's attention away from her. But it didn't work quite the way he hoped.

"Because rumor has it you plan to shut down our

favorite form of entertainment, and this one here is the one who brings in the crowds. Now, I admit, I could just take her back with me fair and square and start my own rodeo, but this is such a perfect central location, and you've already got all of this." Merrick opened his arms wide and took in the specially made barn and arena. "Why go through all of the expense and trouble to build my own when it's all right here?"

Keegan saw his way out. "Well now, who the hell told you that?" Relaxing his body one muscle at a time, he removed his hat, wiped the sweat from his brow, ran his fingers through his hair, and stuck it back on his head. Damn Texas heat. It was practically winter, for fuck's sake.

Merrick cocked his head, a faint shade of interest crossing his features.

However, with Merrick's own words, he'd seen a way to get Bitsy out of harm's way, and he was grabbing those reins. "Why don't we get this one back to her cell—where I was taking her before you two interrupted me—and you and I can go sit on the porch and chew this over?" He glanced back at Corrina. "Maybe Cor will even make us some of her famous lemonade."

"You're putting this one in a cell?" Merrick pointed at Bitsy with his thumb. His tone told Keegan he was nowhere near convinced.

"Why else do you think I brought her here?" Bitsy's sharp intake of breath stabbed through his chest like a knife. He couldn't look at her, couldn't reassure her. Merrick's sharp eyes would catch the slightest nuance, and the game would be up.

"You don't really expect us to believe this?" Corrina

scoffed. "I saw you leave her outside the barn while you came in to get her father."

"All part of the ruse. Her father was the way I got her back here. But this female isn't just 'spunky', she's smart. She wasn't about to just walk into this barn again. And no one was around to help me keep a hold of her." He looked between Corrina and Merrick, a wide grin on his face that was painful to sustain. "Y'all just made my job a hell of a lot easier by having no guard and no key. I didn't even have to lie to her."

Merrick climbed off the motorcycle and approached Keegan and Bitsy. Reaching into his pocket, he pulled out a set of keys and tossed them to Keegan.

Keegan caught them automatically.

"Then go lock her up," Merrick said with a challenge in his eyes. "We'll wait here."

He was testing him. Touching the brim of his hat, Keegan turned and took Bitsy by the arm. Even though he braced himself, the force of the anger and betrayal on her face hit him hard. But the others were watching, and so he just smirked at her and led her to the cells in the back of the building.

Once they were out of the arena, Bitsy dug in her heels and he had no choice but to stop.

"What the fuck do you think you're doing?" Her dark eyes pleaded with him to tell her it was all some kind of huge misunderstanding.

Keegan glanced over his shoulder to make sure no one had followed them before he put his finger to his lips. Leaning in, he whispered right next to her ear, "Trust me, ittybit."

"What if you can't get me out?"

She only mouthed the words, but Keegan heard them loud and clear. They were the same words clanging around in his head. But it wouldn't happen. He'd make sure of it. With a tug on her arm, he hurried her through the door that led to the cell room.

Bitsy allowed him to usher her inside, her heart pounding so hard he could hear it over his own. But as soon as she crossed the threshold, she came to a screeching halt.

"Dad!"

Keegan released her, and she rushed to one of the males in the first cell as the other male and female inside with him looked on with curiosity. They grabbed each other up through the bars, and he heard Bitsy's sob the same time he saw a tear run down the grinning cheek of the male he knew to be her father. She had his dark hair and eyes, and the same dimple on the left side of her cheek when she smiled.

The male pushed her away, the grin of relief falling from his rugged face. "Bits? What the fuck are you doing here?"

Keegan almost smiled. It appeared she also had his mouth. He inserted the key into the empty middle cell and opened the door. He didn't say anything, just waited.

After a moment, Bitsy noticed him standing there. She hesitated a second before she swiped at the tears on her cheeks. Then she straightened her spine and marched inside.

Keegan gently closed the door behind her, shutting off his heart with the turn of the key.

CHAPTER 18

Bitsy watched Keegan leave before she turned back to the man who had taught her everything she knew about family.

Her father smiled and reached through the bars again, taking her by the shoulders and pulling her in for one of his spine-crushing hugs.

When he finally released her, Bitsy gave him a wop on the shoulder. "Where the hell have you been, Dad?"

"First, tell me how your mom is. Is she safe?"

"Mom is fine. She's in Seattle with Bronaugh."

"Oh, thank the gods. And Bronaugh found you both—"

"Yeah, she found us here and got us out."

"By herself?"

Bitsy could tell by her father's tone he was thinking the worst. The only way Bro would've been able to get them out of a situation like this would have been if she'd embraced her dark side. As a an *olc*, or Dark Fae, the iron wouldn't affect her and she would be more powerful than any werewolf. She'd also be batshit crazy. "She had a little help of the wolfy sort."

"Does this *help* happen to be the reason they are both in Seattle?"

Her father was nothing if not astute. "His name is Marc Kincaid. He's a shifter. But he's nothing like these assholes." And at the moment, she was including Keegan in that group. "He's from Seattle, and he's Scottish, as are the other members of his pack. They've been here in the states for quite a long time. Marc's pack leader, Cedric, has quite the reputation, but I don't really get it. He seems like a big teddy bear to me." She shrugged. "Mom has them all twisted right around her little finger. Even Lucian. The grumpy one who hates Fae."

Her father grinned, and his voice was warm with affection when he said, "I wouldn't doubt it. She has a way about her."

Bitsy suddenly felt like she was intruding, as she almost always did around her parents, who were still very much in love. "So, long story short, Bronaugh met Marc while she was nosing around this pack looking for me and mom. They fell in instant lust with each other."

"That's usually how it starts." He looked at her expectantly.

Bitsy frowned, wondering what he was getting at. "And even though Marc was down here trying to finagle an alliance of sorts between this pack and his, Bronaugh got caught by some of the idiots here and thrown in here with us. Unlike *some* people I know—and I'm not talking about you, Dad—he couldn't just stand by and let Bronaugh be hurt, so he saved us all to be with her. He also killed the biggest douchebag of them all and fucked up any chance of goodwill between the packs. But then I agreed to come down here, and Keegan—the one who brought me in here—agreed to the alliance if I would help him find more soul suckers for his rodeo. In exchange, if we found you, he would let you come home with me. And we did. First try." She stopped to take a breath. Her father didn't need to know the real reason he wanted her back. "Which was good, because I had no intention of helping him wrangle any more of our kind into such torture."

Her father had eyed her strangely as she babbled along. "Are you going to tell me what's going on with you and the shifter who brought you in here?"

Bitsy looked away, not that hiding would do any good. She should've known she wouldn't be able to gloss over it that easy. Still, she said it anyway. "Nothing. There's nothing going on."

Her father studied her a moment, then said, "Okay." He took a deep breath and rubbed his forehead.

The female behind him coughed, and he jumped, like he just remembered they were there. "Oh, yes! Guess I should introduce you all, as it seems we'll be spending some time together in such intimate quarters." Her father waved the others forward. When they'd joined him at the bars, he said, "This is Steven and Alice. We met…oh, well, that's a long story for another day. Suffice it to say, they helped me out, and once I was able, they even came with me to search for Bronaugh. We didn't make if very far at all, when we were caught one night, not very far from where I'd left you and your mother."

"Caught by whom?" Bitsy asked him.

"Merrick? I think his name is? I only heard it in passing from others. He kept us in a cave somewhere in the mountains. The entryway was constantly guarded. They had guns with some type of special bullets. There were four of us when we were first caught. Another male was with us. Steven's brother. He was very young. Very brave. And very rash."

Bitsy had a very good idea what had happened to the other Fae male.

He cleared his throat. "Anyway, today we were brought here, to this place, where we were immediately thrown into these cells." He looked around at the iron bars. "They don't do much for us, do they?"

"Nope. Not much at all."

A shout echoed down the passageway and hit the closed door to their room.

Bitsy's heart stuttered, then stopped completely for a moment before it resumed pounding in her chest so fast she got lightheaded and had to sit down. She knew that voice. And it was rarely raised. The fact that it was now didn't bode well for her. Or for him.

Her father knelt beside her, but she couldn't hear what he was saying. Then the building shook around them, dust falling from the ceiling like it used to when the bikes would roar through the arena during the rodeo, and they all glanced up automatically before quickly lowering their heads to keep the dust out of their eyes. After a minute, everything settled down again.

"Who the hell was that?" Alice cried.

"That was our only chance out of this joint," Bitsy told her.

CHAPTER 19

After locking Bitsy away where she wouldn't be harmed, at least for now, Keegan returned to the arena to find Stone leaning back against the railing, the heel of one booted foot hooked on the bottom rung, arms crossed over his blue plaid shirt.

He was alone. Merrick and Corrina were gone.

Unsure where his loyalties were now, Keegan approached him with caution. "I was wondering where you were."

"I've been around. Staying out of sight, like you said."

"Were you able to overhear anything else?"

Pushing away from the railing, Stone pushed his black felt cowboy hat back on his head. "I did. I was hidden outside when Merrick and Corrina left. They were having quite a...heated discussion." He grinned. "And not the good kind."

"So, are you gonna stand there and flirt with me, or are you gonna fill me in on what's going on?"

"Where's Bitsy?"

Keegan glanced around, unsure what eyes may be watching, or what ears might be listening.

"It's cool, Keegan. Merrick and Corrina are back at the house. Everyone else is still out. It's just you and me."

Keegan studied his friend. He had no reason not to believe what he said, and his instincts were telling him they were truly alone. Stone might be the world's only hybrid, but he'd never been anything but straight up and loyal. Keegan hoped that still held true. "I locked her in one of the cells. I was trying to convince Merrick I had no intention of stopping the rodeo. I told him it had all been a trick to get her back here. She always was the main attraction, after all." The words left a sour taste in his mouth.

"If I were you, I wouldn't trust your own pack right now, either. Merrick's been giving them an earful since he got here." Stone paused and looked at Keegan intently. "You know he's here to take over your pack, right?"

"I'm aware." He didn't go into more detail. Though he wanted to trust Stone, he was still feeling him out. He needed to be sure.

"What are you gonna do about it?"

"What can I do? I'll have to fight him."

"He also put out the call for the rodeo tonight. Packs are coming from all over to see the new Faerie blood." Stone scratched his head beneath his hat. "And now your Faerie is in there, too."

"Her name is Bitsy," Keegan told him between clenched teeth.

Stone started to roll his eyes, much like Bitsy did, but then he stopped and his dark eyes were intense on Keegan's face. "I apologize, man. Sincerely. Bitsy. Bitsy is in there."

Keegan paced away again, thinking. "I need to get her and her father out of here. And I need to do it now." Spinning on his boot heel, he headed back toward the hall that would take him to the cell room.

Stone grabbed his arm as he passed him. "No. That's not a good idea, man. It's a bad idea. A terrible idea."

Keegan stopped and narrowed his eyes, suspicion sharpening his senses and making his skin tingle. "Why is it a bad idea to save the female I care about?"

Releasing his arm, Stone held up his hands, palms out. "Just hear me out, Keegan. And then, whatever you decide, I'll stand with you."

The air he didn't realize he was holding released from his lungs on a loud exhale. "Go on, then."

"I know it's hard for you to leave her in there, but if you go get her out now, you'll have no choice but to run. You'll be called a coward. Merrick will say you ran from his challenge. You'll lose all credibility as an Alpha, or even as a werewolf."

But Keegan was already shaking his head. "I'll get her somewhere safe. I'll get her back to Seattle, and then I'll come back here and settle the score with Merrick."

"You and I both know that's not how it works, man. You won't make it to Austin before you'll be taken out by the other wolves, thinking they're protecting their true Alpha—Merrick."

"I'll have to take that chance. At least Bitsy will be safe."

"And you'll be dead. Who will continue to keep her safe then? Cuz you know damn well Merrick won't let her go off and live in peace. Not after this. He'll bring her back here just to prove a point."

Much as Keegan hated to admit it, Stone was right. Running with her would only put her life in more danger, because as much as he'd like to believe otherwise, the truth of the matter was, for the first time in his life, he may not win this fight.

He went to rub his forehead, but his hat was in the way. In a fit of emotion, he flung it from his head as he released a shout of frustration, then kicked out at the bars of the cage surrounding the arena. The metal bent under the force of his anger but didn't break.

Stone didn't try to stop him, didn't try to calm him down. He just stood by silently while Keegan tried—unsuccessfully—to take out the barn single-handedly.

When he was finished, Keegan stood with his head bowed and his hands low on his hips, breathing hard. He never should have brought Bitsy back here. It was a stupid thing to do. Of course, he hadn't known what Merrick had been planning. But he should have. He'd gotten lazy, gotten too secure in his position, gotten too chummy with the other pack leaders neighboring him. And he'd forgotten to keep an eye on his back. They came for the entertainment. It was an escape from the boredom that came with peace. They weren't friends. As he'd explained to Bitsy, shifters were happiest when they had something to fight for. When they had a purpose. Even if they had to create that purpose themselves.

If they could create a war, even better. And that's exactly what Merrick was trying to do.

He wasn't going to allow Bitsy and her father to be caught in the crossfire.

"So, what now?" Stone asked him.

"Guess we're having a rodeo tonight."

Hours passed, and Bitsy had curled up in the corner of her cell as close as she could get to her father. They held hands through the bars.

No one had come in to tell them what all the commotion had been about earlier. No one had brought them anything to eat or drink, or even to poke at them with cattle prods like they did the first time she was here.

But worse than that, Bitsy had no idea if Keegan was still here, or if he was hurt, or even worse—if he was still alive.

Her father had tried again to get her to talk about him, but she couldn't give him answers to questions she didn't know herself. Things like how she felt about the werewolf who had allowed her to be dragged around his arena behind a motorcycle with a chain wrapped around her neck, then claimed he had feelings for her, then brought her back to the one place where it had all began using her father as bait. In retrospect, it had been entirely too easy for him to get her right back into this cell.

And like an idiot, she'd walked right in. She'd taken a chance on him. And she'd lost.

She did, however, find out the cells had been empty when her father and his friends had been brought here. She wondered idly what had happened to the two soul suckers who had been here with her and her mom. Not that she missed them grunting and hissing and smashing their heads into the bars.

The door opened and one of the younger shifters came inside carrying two brown paper grocery bags. Bitsy recognized him from her last visit. His name was Lance? Leroy? Something like that. But more importantly, he was part of Keegan's pack, which meant they were back at the ranch house and maybe he would know what had happened.

"Hey," she said when he came in. "What's going on out there?"

Non-descript hazel eyes lifted to hers and narrowed with distrust. He didn't respond as he grabbed a cattle prod from the back table and approached the cells. "Back away from the door," he told her father.

The three Fae in the next cell obediently moved away from the door, and the young shifter unlocked it and gave them one of the bags he'd brought inside. He closed and re-locked their door, then moved to Bitsy's cell.

She backed away from the door without his having to tell her. She knew the routine. If she didn't, a nice jolt with that prod and a good kick would get her to the back of the cell. "What happened out there earlier?" she asked again. "Did Keegan and Merrick fight? Is Keegan still alive?"

The shifter threw her bag inside and started closing the door.

As he lowered the prod, Bitsy took her chance and rushed the opening. Ignoring her father's shout of panic, she threw her body forward, wincing as the young wolf tried to slam it shut and she got caught in between. Grabbing the wrist that held the prod, she struggled to keep the tip away from her until he was forced to look at her. "Just tell me if he's fucking alive," she gritted out.

The kid suddenly released the door, and as Bitsy fell forward, he used his free hand to shove her back into her cell. Before she could get to her feet, he slammed it shut and twisted the lock. Before he turned to leave, he paused. "He's alive. For now."

Bitsy stood in the middle of the cell, breathing hard, not quite sure what to do with that knowledge. She'd been certain he and Merrick had fought, and that Keegan had lost. Because if he'd won, why was she still in this cell? Why hadn't he at least come to see her? "I'm a fucking idiot," she whispered to herself.

The door slammed shut behind the kid as he made haste out of the room. The noise shook her from her stupor, and Bitsy felt the numbness she'd been living with for the past few hours drain out of her. It left behind a sharp ache that stole her breath.

"I'm sure he has a good reason for not coming back for you yet," her dad said softly.

She sucked in a breath. "Because he fucking lied to me?"

"We don't know that, Bits."

"Yes," she said as her eyes filled with damning tears. "We do."

"Bitsy—"

"I've been such a fool, Dad." She tried to smile, but had the feeling it looked more like a watery grimace. "After everything he'd done to me and Mom and Bronaugh, I still came back here. I still gave him my trust"—and much more—"and he lied to me. He even got me to come back to this ranch of my own free will. Hell, I walked right into the barn, right into this fucking cell." She scowled at the floor. "And the asshat has my necklace."

She felt her father's hand on her shoulder. "You did all of this for me. Don't feel guilty about that, Bits. And I can make you a new necklace."

But had she? Finding her father was the most important reason she'd come back, that was true. But it didn't explain the flutters in her stomach when she'd heard her return to Texas was the only way Keegan would agree to the alliance. It was her own stupid fault she misconstrued the reason why.

Because her stupid body was drawn to him like a black hole. And he knew it. And he'd used that attraction against her.

"It's not your fault, Bits. It's mine."

Pulled from her thoughts, she turned to stare at her father. "How do you figure that?"

"Because I am your fucking father. I should be protecting you, not the other way around." He rubbed his forehead again. "I never should have left you and your mother to go look for Bronaugh. I just—" His hand fell to his side. "I just couldn't stand the thought she believed being apart from us was what any of us wanted. I never would have forgiven myself if I hadn't at least tried and anything had happened to her."

Bitsy went to her father and took his hands between the bars. "Daddy, there's no need to apologize. Bronaugh is my sister in everything but blood. If you hadn't gone after her, I would have. And then who knows what trouble we would've gotten ourselves into?"

Her teasing tone worked, and he chuckled as he squeezed her hands. "Something much worse than a rodeo, that's for sure."

"Absofuckinglutely." She grinned back at him.

Her teasing was cut short when the door opened again and a lanky shifter Bitsy didn't recognize came in. Everyone got quiet as he grabbed the cattle prod before coming over to open the door to her father's cell.

"Let's go. All of you. Don't make any sudden movements, or I'll fry your asses before you can get two feet away."

Bitsy rushed to the bars. "Wait! Stop! Where are you taking them?"

The shifter grinned at her. His right eyetooth was gold. It glinted in the light of the fluorescent bulb. "It's show time, girlie. Don't worry, I'm coming for you next."

"What are you talking about?"

Gold Tooth didn't answer her as he ushered the three Fae out to the hall that led to the arena.

Bitsy's heart stuttered in her chest. Frantically, she knelt down to open the brown bag they hadn't had time to open yet, searching for something—anything—that would help her.

The contents inside warmed her blood.

Her bag contained food, yes. A sandwich and a water bottle. But it also contained something else. Something that glinted in the bottom corner of the bag. So small, she'd almost missed it.

It was her necklace.

The tree pendant her father had forged for her from pure silver was dull and covered in dirt. Bitsy purposely kept her mind blank as she popped the cap off the water bottle and washed it off until it shined. Then she refastened it around her neck. The metal was cold, the weight of the pendant heavy. But once it was on, her soul felt instantly lighter, because this was no ordinary necklace. It had been made especially for her, and blessed by an elder, to keep her safe.

As it would to whoever was wearing it.

So, if Keegan had been wearing this pendant, she knew the young male hadn't lied to her earlier. He was still alive. And he'd sent it to her to let her know.

But without it, she had the feeling he wouldn't be much longer.

The door opened and old Gold Tooth came back in. "You're turn, girlie." Holding the cattle prod out in front of him, he opened the door.

Bitsy obediently exited her cell and walked ahead of him to the door. She wasn't about to give him any reason to jab her with that thing. And despite his greasy appearance, he didn't appear to be the sort who was cruel without reason.

As they approached the entrance to the arena, she heard the familiar rumble of the crowd. It rose to a roar when she was led out into the chute to join the others. A group of males shouted words of encouragement to her from the bleachers above. Money quickly changed hands as bets were made.

Who knew she was so fucking popular?

The amusement fell from her face as someone very familiar to her strolled out into the center of arena. Lifting his arms, he attempted to quiet the crowd. Her eyes wandered from his buckskin hat, down his open shirt and rugged jeans, to the worn boots that covered his feet.

For a brief moment, she felt like he'd punched her right in the gut.

Bitsy shook her head hard. She was hallucinating. That had to be it. Keegan wouldn't be out there. He wouldn't do this to her. Not after all they'd been through. Not after the way he'd held her.

"You have your necklace back." Her father's voice sounded far away, though he stood right beside her. "What does that mean?"

"I have no fucking idea." And she really didn't. Was it to tell her not to worry? That this was all part of some heroic plan to free them all? Or was it to tell her he didn't care?

"Doesn't look so smug now, does he?" Alice said.

Bitsy frowned, thinking she was talking about Keegan. Smug was not a normal expression for him. Well, usually. Following the direction of her stare, she saw Merrick standing just outside the chute. His face was flushed, the muscles in his jaw flexed from the tension. Alice was right. He didn't look happy at all.

As Keegan welcomed everyone to the rodeo, they watched as Merrick clenched his fists at his sides.

Gold Tooth let himself out of the chute and said something in his ear. Merrick nodded, then strode out to join Keegan in the center of the arena.

"What the hell is going on?" Steve asked.

Bitsy didn't think he really expected a response, so she didn't give him one.

Keegan watched as Merrick approached him. He didn't smile or give any other form of greeting.

Merrick didn't stop until they stood toe to toe. He said something to Keegan, and Keegan responded with a lift of his eyebrow and a smile for the crowd.

This just seemed to piss Merrick off more. With his finger in Keegan's face, he leaned in, spitting angry words at him.

Bitsy strained to hear what the two Alphas were saying over the low rumble of the crowd. They were both straining into each other now, not touching, their bodies tensing against the weight of their words. Stone went to stand on Keegan's right, as Gold Tooth did for Merrick.

She wondered what Keegan was about. Was he trying to save face in front of his pack?

Maybe he was bargaining with Merrick for her.

Maybe he didn't want her.

Maybe it had nothing to do with her at all.

All these thoughts ran through Bitsy's head as she watched the two werewolves in the center of the arena.

"Can you hear what they're saying?" her father asked.

Bitsy shook her head. "But don't get your hopes up, Dad." She glanced around at the bleachers full of shifters from every neighboring county. "As you can see, this rodeo is the main form of entertainment around here. Even if, by some miracle, they call a halt to it, the crowd will likely kill us in an angry stampede."

Something touched her arm, and she turned to see her father staring at her intently. "I'm so sorry, honey. I'm so sorry I left you and your mother unprotected."

She gave him a sad smile. "It's not your fault, Dad. We should have been more careful, but we'd gotten too comfortable. We didn't even notice when they snuck up on us. It's our own fault we got into this mess. I'm just glad Mom isn't here now." Giving her attention back to the two males in the center of the arena, she was surprised to see them in a silent stand off.

Merrick leaned in, said something quickly in Keegan's ear.

Keegan's expression went ice cold.

Stone stepped forward, his body stiff with anger, but Keegan held up his hand and shut him down. He glanced over at her, and Bitsy met his gaze, but she couldn't read anything in it. His mouth tightened, then he gave Merrick a jerky nod.

Calling for silence once again, Keegan called out to the crowd, "Merrick will take over from here, as I'm needed elsewhere." Without another glance in her direction, he strode from the arena.

Bitsy lost him in the crowd, unsure whether he stuck around or had left the premises entirely.

As the next "event" was announced and eager young

shifters volunteered to participate, Bitsy flung out a curse. "That fucking bastard."

"There must be a good explanation for this," her father argued. "I see how that male looks at you, Bitsy. He cares about you. I refuse to believe he'll just stand there and allow this to happen."

"And yet...he is."

CHAPTER 21

Someone called to him, but Keegan barely noticed over the ringing in his ears as he rushed down one of the trails away from the barn and the commotion going on inside.

"Keegan! What the fuck, man?"

A heavy hand gripped his shoulder and spun him around. Keegan lowered his chin and growled deep in his throat.

Stone took one look at his face and retreated a few steps, but he wasn't completely put off by Keegan's warning. "What are you doing? What did he say to you?"

"You shouldn't be out here in the open."

"No one will see me. Now, fill me in."

"I thought of a way to keep the rodeo from happening, and still satisfy the crowd." He had to force the words out past the knot of rage and helplessness in his chest. "I had it all figured out."

"You were going to challenge him. You were going to be the entertainment."

"Yes. I hoped you were somewhere close by, and you would get Bitsy and the others out of there while the fight was going on."

"Keegan, we discussed this—"

"It would've worked."

Stone rubbed the back of his neck. "Not if you'd lost."

"I wouldn't have lost. Not when I have so much to fucking live for." His skin felt too loose, sliding over muscles beginning to swell with the urge to shift. He took a deep breath. "I just wanted you to take them back to the hotel until I could come for them. I wouldn't be able to concentrate with her there, in the midst of everything, watching."

Hands on his hips, Stone lowered his head. He looked up with a deep inhale. "So, what happened?"

Keegan had to take a few more breaths before he was able to speak. "Merrick knew. Somehow, he fucking *knew* what I was up to. He told me his guys were prepared to remove her head from her body if I tried anything." A sound that was half disgust and half amazement burst from his lungs. "He said if I didn't leave the arena, he would gut her right in front of me. He said he considered it worth the loss to keep things on his terms."

"That guy is seriously fucked up."

"Well, I imagine it would get downright boring spending so much time alone in the mountains with nothing to do but jack off and chase rabbits on the full moon."

"You're joking at a time like this?"

"Yeah, I fucking am. It's that, or go back in there and challenge him anyway. And take the chance that Bitsy could die in front of my eyes." He searched Stone's face. "He's got me by the fucking balls, Stone."

The sound of motorcycles tearing across the arena rent the air. Unable to stand still, Keegan began to prowl back and forth. "She's tough. You said it yourself. She'll make it through tonight." He searched Stone's face, needing confirmation.

"She will." His head whipped around toward the direction of the barn. "Someone's coming."

"Bitsy…"

"I got her." Fast as a vampire, whose blood he carried, he was gone.

And Keegan was left alone.

A few seconds later, he heard footsteps.

"Ah, here you are. I hope I didn't completely kill our friendship by ruining all of your grandiose plans."

"Always so polite, Merrick. Aren't you?" Keegan said.

It wasn't meant as a compliment, but Merrick only smirked. "Well, there's no need to be uncivil about matters."

The sound of the hundreds of shifters applauding and stomping their feet drifted through the sparse trees, and Keegan's heart stuttered.

"Don't worry. Your little Faerie is fine. She's a fighter. A few turns around the arena won't hurt her. Much." Merrick gave him a wink.

Keegan felt something detonate within him. As his body began to shift, he could barely get the words out. "I challenge you, Merrick." Bones snapped in his face. Muscles stretched and grew under loose skin. "For Alpha." It was the last thing he said before the words were lost in a haze of pain.

In response to the challenge, Merrick also began to shift. His Alpha nature left him with no other choice but to fight. He didn't even have time to remove his clothes before he collapsed to the ground, his body grossly distorted.

The sound of breaking bones and the moist suction of muscles separating and re-attaching filled the air. Merrick had barely gotten to his feet again when Keegan threw his head back and howled into the night.

With teeth bared, the two wolves threw themselves at each other, both going for the throat. Neither gaining the upper hand, they separated and circled each other a few times before Keegan launched at him again.

Merrick was tough, much tougher than his appearance let on, and it only took a few seconds for Keegan to realize the chances of his winning this throw down were sketchy at best. More than once, the only thing that kept him on his feet was the thought of Bitsy, and all he was fighting for. Not only the position of Alpha, but a life. A life with her. And how that life would never happen if he lost.

Standing on their hind legs, the two wolves struggled, each trying to get the advantage over the other. Then it happened. Keegan's paw slipped on the blood-soaked fur of Merrick's chest. If he'd been thinking straight, he would have recognized the error and corrected it. But it was a stroke of luck for Merrick, and Keegan went down.

Stumbling at first, Merrick immediately regrouped and went in for the fatal bite. Dipping his head, he got a good grip around Keegan's throat and flipped him onto his back.

Twisting his head back and forth, Keegan tried to force Merrick to release him from his jaws, but he couldn't break his hold. Grimly, he waited to feel the sting of his teeth as he sank them into the artery.

Thoughts of Bitsy filled his head through the haze of pain—her soft, warm skin and taunting mouth. That mouth that begged for his kisses even as she damned his soul with her words. Fear flooded his senses, not for himself, but for her. He'd asked her to trust him. He'd promised her she would be safe.

He had failed her.

Cool air stung the wound in his throat as Merrick's teeth ripped through his fur and skin. For a moment, he lay there on his back, frozen, not comprehending what was happening. He could suddenly breathe again as the weight from his opponent's paws left his chest. And when Keegan managed to flip over and struggle to his feet, he saw why.

Corrina had followed them and knocked Merrick off him. She stood in front of Keegan now in full wolf form, shielding him with her body, head low, teeth bared in a snarl, as she protected her Alpha.

Merrick paced back and forth in front of her, blood dripping from his brown muzzle and bared teeth. But in the end, he couldn't bring himself to hurt her. Throwing his head back, he released a howl of rage and frustration, then he ran into the brush surrounding the house.

A few seconds ticked by before Corrina swung her

grey head around. Her white eyes roamed over Keegan, before she, too, ran off.

Unable to hold himself upright anymore, Keegan fell to his front knees and toppled over onto his side. He stayed there, in a world of hurt, until he was able to shift back. His face burned as he gathered up his torn clothes and stumbled back to the house.

He should have died. It was dishonorable not to die in the fight for Alpha. It was unheard of. Corrina had taken that away, and it took him the entire trip back to the house to get over his pride and be grateful she had given him another chance.

It was hard, but he managed to get over himself. He would right things with Merrick. And next time, he would not make the same mistakes.

Once, right before he went inside, he looked toward the sounds of the rodeo, but he turned away. Part of it was still pride, and he'd readily admit that. He didn't want her to see him beaten down and bloody. The other part of it was caution. He didn't know where Merrick was, and he didn't know whose side his pack would be on. He couldn't take the chance of barging in there and removing Bitsy, not without knowing they wouldn't be hunted by Merrick. Not without knowing she wouldn't be harmed.

Stone was in there, somewhere. And that was good. Because in the shape he was in right now, there was no way in hell he'd be able to protect her.

He could only imagine how she felt about him right now. For all she knew, he'd just walked away and left her there, and was too much of a coward to even stay and watch this time. It would shock the hell out of him if she wanted him now, or if she ever really did. Keegan accepted that. He had let her down. But somehow, some way, he would keep his promise to her, and get her and her father back to Seattle. And if Merrick took him out in the process, so be it.

Luckily, no one was in the ranch house to witness his shame as he painfully climbed the stairs to his room, naked, bruised, and bleeding. His left arm hung awkwardly from his shoulder and blood dripped from his face and right thigh, leaving a trail on the floor.

The last thing he remembered was falling onto his bed as pain racked his body.

CHAPTER 22

"Keegan. Come on, man. You gotta get up."

His bones rattled as someone shook him hard. "What? Stop! Fuck." The last ended on a moan as Keegan shoved away the hands and bolted to an upright position. His head swam, and he couldn't see at first, but as his eyes adjusted, he realized he wasn't actually blind from the knock in the head he'd been dealt. It was just dark outside.

Something sticky glued his hair to his head above his temple, and he tried to wipe it away, but couldn't lift his left arm.

"You gotta get up, Keegan."

The voice was familiar. "Stone?" He searched the dark for his friend's face, and finally spotted the glow of his eyes to his left. The rest of it slowly came into focus. "What are you still doing here?"

"I've been around." Grabbing Keegan's left wrist, he braced his other hand on his shoulder. With a pull and a twist, he put the arm back in the socket.

Keegan grunted with the sudden pain. When it was over, he tried moving his arm. It was sore, but it worked. "Thanks."

"Anytime. Now come on, we gotta get out of here."

"Fuck. What time is it? Where is everyone?" He froze. "Where's Bitsy? You're supposed to be with her."

"Don't you hear them?"

Keegan quieted his breathing and listened. He heard the rumble of engines and then a jovial shout, answered by another. "What's happening?" He found Stone's shoulders and gripped them tight. "Is it over? Are they leaving?"

Stone took the opportunity to grab him around the ribs and lift him from the bed. "Can you walk?"

Keegan took stock of his body as his mind caught up to what was happening. He felt like he'd been caught in a stampede. And he was naked. "I fought Merrick."

"I kinda figured that's what happened. Except imagine my surprise when I see him walking around and, and when I go look for you, I find you up here, all beaten and bloody, but still breathing."

Keegan swayed on his feet and Stone reached out to steady him. His memory was flooding back. "I lost the fight. His teeth were around my throat." His hand gripped his neck like a wolf's jaw. "But Cor saved me. She protected me. Instead of taking her out, Merrick took off. She followed him."

"Well, that's the good news. The bad news is, the lover's quarrel is over and they seem to have made up. Merrick is back and so is Corrina. The neighboring packs are starting to pack up and leave. Which means, if you want to stay breathing, we gotta go, and we gotta go *now*. We can blend in with everyone as they leave."

"I need clothes."

Stone braced him against the wall, then rummaged through his drawers and pulled out jeans and socks and a tank. He helped Keegan dress before leaving him again to find his spare boots in the closet.

"Okay," Stone said once he'd helped him get his boots on. "Let's go get your girl and get the fuck out of here."

But Keegan slapped his hands against the doorframe, stalling. "I can't just run away like a coward, Stone. I need to see this through."

"You go out there right now, Merrick will kill you. Not because he's the better Alpha, but because he's in better shape than you right now."

"If he wins, he wins. At least I'll die an honorable death."

"And what about Bitsy and the others locked in that barn? Will their death be honorable?"

The blood pounded in his aching head, and Keegan suddenly turned on his second in command. "What the fuck do you care?" he snarled. "You don't give a shit about her, or about any of them. You never did."

"No. I don't. But I do give a shit about you, and finally got it through this thick skull of mine that she is yours. Which makes her a part of this pack now. Whatever's left of it."

Mine.

Bitsy is mine.

Keegan felt like the world was spinning around him, yet he was standing perfectly still. "She's mine."

Stone said nothing, and Keegan gripped the front of his shirt.

"Merrick's been planning this all along. He wants to take over the pack. Take over the rodeo."

"And you're going to be the special attraction if we don't get you the hell up outta here. Somewhere where you can recuperate and get your strength back."

Keegan resisted as Stone grabbed his upper arm and tried to steer him from the room. "Bitsy is in there."

"I know. Let me get you out of here, and I'll come back for her as soon as everyone is out of the barn."

"No." In spite of his earlier words, and his many years of loyalty, Keegan wasn't ready to trust him with Bitsy's life.

"It's the only way to do this, man. You're in no condition to—"

"No!"

Stone slapped a hand over his mouth.

The salt of his skin stung an open cut on Keegan's upper lip. He pulled his hand away and immediately lowered his voice. "I can't leave here without her. What if she's hurt?"

"She's tough, Keegan. She survived everything Jace put her through." He paused. "Everything I put her through," he said quietly. "She survived tonight."

But Keegan was already pulling away from him and heading toward the door.

Stone grabbed him by the back of the shirt before he could open the door. "Keegan," he whispered fiercely. "You can't save her. Not right now. Not like this. Merrick *will* kill you this time if you step foot in that arena."

Keegan knocked his hands away. "She'll never forgive me if I leave her there, Stone. And I *need* her to forgive me." But it wasn't just Bitsy's anger he worried about. If he followed Stone's advice, she would understand, hopefully, eventually, why he'd done what he had. And Stone was right. She might be itty, but she was tough. She would survive until he could get to her.

However, Keegan was *not* that strong. He could not leave his female in there another second to be abused and ridiculed by his kind. It had nearly killed him the first time, though somehow, he'd managed to fool everyone. Everyone except Stone, that is. His second in command was the only one he'd let his guard down around. The only one who knew how it had torn Keegan apart to keep the rodeo after Bitsy and her mom had been brought in.

Back then, he'd never done anything about it, afraid of something exactly like this happening. Afraid of mutiny from his pack. Afraid of being challenged.

Now, he didn't give a fuck anymore. "I'm going." Taking Stone's face between his palms, he brought their foreheads together for a moment. "Thank you. For sticking by me."

Stone covered his hands with his own. "I ain't going anywhere, man. If you're going to get her, I'm coming with you. It's you and me."

Keegan pulled back to look him in the eye. "We may not come out of that arena. You get that."

White teeth glowed in the darkness as Stone grinned. "Oh, I don't know about that. Merrick hasn't seen me at my worst."

A flash of hope hit Keegan. Though it hurt, he returned Stone's smile. "And maybe he's underestimated you."

"Let's hope so, man. Let's hope so."

"But if Merrick and I get into it again, you don't jump in on anything. Understood? What will happen, will happen."

"As long as he plays it fair, I won't interfere. You have my word. And I'll get Bitsy and her father out of there and back to Seattle. For you, I'll do that, man."

"All right, then. Let's go." Keegan squeezed Stone's shoulder one last time, then turned and carefully opened the bedroom door. The house was quiet, everyone out in the barn for the night's entertainment. Keegan grabbed his last spare hat from the peg by the door on the way out.

They descended the stairs. Keegan didn't bother trying to conceal the sound of his boots on the wooden steps. This was still his fucking house. "Anyone else in the pack still loyal to me that you know of? Or have they all turned?"

"You can count out the younger pups. They're not ballsy enough yet to stand up to someone like Merrick, and ya can't blame them there. It's hard to tell with the others. I think a few of the guys who've been with you forever, like me, will back you up if it comes down to it. Corrina, though…yeah. She's lost to us, man."

"Guess one of us will have to learn how to make our own fucking coffee from now on." The joke fell flat. As they approached the back door, Keegan took a deep, painful breath, then pushed it open. Though his body still ached like a son of a bitch and his head swam with every move he made, no one would know it unless they got all up and personal. He was good at hiding what was really going on with him. It was crucial to survival in his world, and he'd learned from an early age.

"Last chance to change your mind, man," Stone mumbled as they made their way between the trucks and cars sitting with the engines running, waiting their turn to leave. A few doors opened as shifters got out to get a better look at Keegan. Some shut their cars off and fell in behind them, whispering with excitement.

Keegan didn't bother responding to Stone. He was getting Bitsy out of there, whatever it cost him.

As he approached the open wooden door with Stone close on his heels, shifters on their way out to their cars cleared a path to let them through. Heads pressed close together, and murmurs came to his ear. They all wondered what was happening. Tension and excitement filled the air, thick as soup.

Corrina stood at the cage door, waiting for Merrick to come out of the arena, if he were to guess. Her eyes grew white with fear when she saw them coming. But she stood her ground and blocked the entry. "You need to get the hell out of here, Keegan."

Though she was a tall female, Keegan had no trouble seeing over her head and into the arena. And what he saw made his pulse pound until spots danced in front of his eyes.

Bitsy and her father were the only two left in the arena. Their hands and feet were shackled with the iron chains used to hunt and capture their kind and get them back to the ranch, encumbering their movements and further weakening them as they were corralled toward the chute with cattle prods.

As he watched, Bitsy was stuck in the ass by Merrick's second, the one with the gold tooth. The bastard laughed as she yelped, her body stiffening and jerking in pain until he pulled the prod away and she fell to her knees. She swayed like that for a moment before her upper body went down, her face sliding into the dirt, her chained hands unable to stop her from falling.

Merrick stood watching, the corners of his mouth turned up in a smirk.

Shaking with the force of this rage, the pain of his unhealed injuries overridden by the adrenaline rushing through him, Keegan gripped Corrina around the throat and lifted her until only the toes of her boots scraped the dirt below. "Open the *fucking* door."

Though her eyes bulged from her head, and her hands clawed at his arm trying to get him to release her, she still managed to mouth the words, "I won't. He'll kill you."

"One of us has to die tonight, Corrina. And it's gonna be you if you don't open this door."

Tears filled her eyes as she stopped struggling. She shook her head as much as she could within his grip.

"Stone. The lock."

Stone stepped forward and gripped the lock. With little effort, he busted the thick metal with one hand and ripped it from the door.

Keegan tossed Corrina to the side as Stone held the door open for him.

The noise of the crowd rose in excitement as Keegan calmly strolled to the center of the arena where Merrick stood. The air vibrated with the aura of hundreds of tense shifters, already worked up from the night's events.

Merrick must have felt the change in the air. His smile fell abruptly from his face as his eyes searched the remaining crowd, taking in the change of atmosphere. Then he slowly turned. When he saw Keegan approaching him, an expression between disbelief and delight lit up his bruised face. Holding up his hands, he waited until the crowd quieted down. "What are you doing here, Keegan? Come to reveal your shame publicly?"

Hundreds of pairs of eyes weighed on Keegan as the crowd waited for his response. But the only one there he cared about was Bitsy. Without pause, he headed for her.

Merrick stepped in his path. "What are you doing here, Keegan?"

"Why I'm fixin' to get my girl and her people outta here, Merrick."

Merrick barked out a laugh. "I'm not letting you leave here with my biggest attraction."

"Then I guess you should've killed me." Shouldering Merrick out of the way, Keegan continued toward Bitsy, who was struggling to stand.

The noise level increased as all eyes shifted between the two Alphas and put two and two together.

Before he could reach her, two of Merrick's pack cut him off. Stone stepped up to clear them out of the way, but Keegan stopped him with a hand on his arm. "This is gonna go down tonight one way or the other," he muttered. "Might as well be now." Right before he turned around, he whispered, "I'm putting her life in your hands, buddy."

"I got her. And you," Stone replied.

With a nod to Stone, Keegan turned to face Merrick.

"You've got a lot of balls, showing up here."

The other Alpha was as embarrassed as Keegan but was trying to cover it. It showed by the high color in his cheeks and the way he was grinding his teeth so hard Keegan half expected them to crumble from his mouth. Most likely, he'd told no one he'd left Keegan alive, thinking he would slink off in shame as soon as he woke up.

"I think you're a mite confused, Merrick. I've nothing to be ashamed of. You might or might not have beaten me in a fight, but I'm not the one who's been sniffing around another Alpha's pack. I'm not the one who tried to kill off that other Alpha by blowing up his truck instead of challenging him outright like a male of honor."

It suddenly got very quiet.

Skirting around that accusation, Merrick goaded, "You can sing it however you want, try to make me look like the bad guy, but I *am* the male who won the challenge. We both know if it wasn't for Corrina's misplaced affection for you, you would be dead right now."

Keegan pushed his hat back on his head. "True. But I'm not dead, am I." He strolled closer to the other Alpha and lowered his voice. "You have something of mine, Merrick. I want her back."

"Ah, now. It's common knowledge now that you were gonna shut this rodeo down, Keegan. But I refuse to let that happen. And I can't very well just give up my main entertainment. Not after everything I've gone through to get her back here."

It wasn't an admission, but it was close enough. "Then I'll just be *taking* her."

Merrick chuckled. "You can certainly try." Swinging his arms out to the side, he indicated the shifters around them. "Take a look around, my friend. There are plenty of witnesses this time. No one will save you."

"That's all right, because I don't plan on losing."

"Are you challenging me to a rematch? Now? Before you've had a chance to heal from the last ass-whooping I gave you?"

"I am." Backing away, Keegan took off his hat and tossed it to the ground, followed by his boots and shirt. Barefoot, in only his jeans, he announced his intention to the crowd at large. "I challenge you for the Alpha position of my pack *and* yours."

Merrick rested his weight on one leg with his hands on his hips, a deceptively casual pose, and laughed.

But Keegan wasn't to be deterred. "Or maybe it's you who's in no condition to fight, Merrick." With so many witnesses, Merrick also wouldn't be able to figure out a way to cheat. The challenge would be fought fair and square.

Merrick's smile turned bitter cold. "I accept your challenge."

With his quiet acceptance, the arena cleared out as shifters piled back into the bleachers, and money again began flying from hand to hand as bets were made and changed. The Texas pack and the Colorado pack stayed in the arena to bear witness, forming a large circle around the two Alphas.

While Merrick removed his clothes, Keegan allowed

himself one last look at Bitsy. She'd managed to struggle to her feet, and now stood, assisted by her father. Her eyes were huge in her dirty, pixie-like face as she took in all the commotion around them.

He shifted his gaze to her father. The elder male returned his measuring look, then gave him a nod of respect before he pulled his daughter closer to the chute to watch from a safe distance.

Pushing her from his head, he turned away.

"Keegan!"

Bitsy's voice cut through the buzzing between his ears. His eyes clashed with hers, and in the dark depths, he saw pain, confusion, denial—

And concern.

He seared her image into his brain. Then he turned away, removed his jeans, and prepared to shift.

CHAPTER 23

The complete and utter loathing that had been growing within Bitsy since Keegan walked away had only intensified with every piece of skin she lost in the dirt and every breath-stealing shock she received from the cattle prods—not to mention the shame of being roped and tossed about like cattle.

But those feelings drained out of her like dirty dishwater as she watched him with Merrick.

His face was badly bruised and swollen. Dried blood stuck pieces of his hair to his forehead and streaked his face and neck. He walked like his boots were too small. And he held his left arm protectively against his side.

Merrick had returned beat up, but to her sensitive eyes, Keegan looked like he should be in a hospital bed.

She had assumed the worst when he hadn't come back, and she'd hated him for it. For everything. For enticing her back down to this godforsaken state. For seducing her body with his alluring masculinity, and her mind with his heartfelt apologies. For giving her hope.

Only to walk away again.

Only to leave her forever.

After the first event had started, when Merrick had followed him out and returned alone, she'd known what had happened. The rules of shifters were simple: the only way to win the position of Alpha was to kill your opponent. There was no quarter. There was no mercy.

It was a miracle that he was alive. And now he was fucking it all up by giving Merrick another shot at him.

Disgusting sounds filled the air as the two Alphas shifted into their wolf forms. Bitsy turned away from the sight to find Stone facing off against Gold Tooth. She was slightly surprised to see his upper lip drawn back, exposing long fangs not of the wolf type, even as he growled deep in his chest in warning—very wolf-like.

Gold Tooth smirked, but he held up his hands and backed away.

Stone kept an eye on him until he'd joined the rest of his pack off to the side, then he turned to her and her father. "Where are the other two?" Grabbing Bitsy's chains first, he held the cuff around her wrist with one hand and yanked the chain off with the other, then did the same with her other wrist and her ankles.

"Back in the cells," her father told him, holding out his arms. "They're not...um, they couldn't..." He dwindled off, his expression speaking volumes.

"Can they walk out of here if we have to leave quick?"

"Probably," Bitsy whispered.

"More or less," her father said at the same time.

Stone didn't look pleased by the answer, but he said no more. Turning his attention to the two wolves now circling each other in the center of the arena, he took up a protective stance beside Bitsy and her father.

Bitsy had no love for this one, but what she did know was he was completely loyal to his Alpha. "What happened earlier? Did they fight?" she asked. "Why is Keegan doing this?"

"It's the only way to get you out of here."

"But, they already fought, yes?"

"Yes."

"And they're both still alive?"

Stone spared her a quick glance. "Corrina interrupted the fight." He didn't say anything else, but he didn't have to. His expression was indecipherable, but his dark eyes told her all she needed to know.

"Keegan lost." Her voice was barely above a whisper.

Surprisingly, or maybe not so surprisingly, considering what he was, Stone heard her. "He did."

Which meant he had come back to die, instead of taking the second chance at life and running. He could have left the state, left the country, started over somewhere else. Started a new pack, perhaps.

But instead, he'd come back to avenge his honor.

"I know what you're thinking," Stone told her. "But you're wrong. He's not here for himself. He's here for you." He didn't sound like he agreed with his Alpha's decision. "He has to win; it's the only way you won't be hunted."

She cringed as the two wolves flew at each other. Blood sprayed one side of the circle. She couldn't tell whose it was. But it only aroused the shifters standing in its path, and they shifted their weight back and forth, eyes on the fight. "Why?"

"Don't you know? That male is head over paws for your little Faerie ass."

Her father cleared his throat.

Stone touched the brim of his hat. "No offense."

Bitsy tore her eyes from the fury of fur and teeth and blood happening in front of her. "You don't know that."

"Oh, but I do. He always has been. From the moment he saw you. He made me promise to get you both out of here and back to Cedric in Seattle, whatever the outcome." He speared her with his dark eyes. "And I intend to do just that, no matter what goes down here. Because I promised. Hopefully, they'll be grateful enough to take me in, and protect all of us from Merrick. Because there's no way in hell I'm staying here."

"You don't think he'll win."

"Do you?"

"Yes," she answered without hesitation, and she was surprised to find she meant it. He would win. He had to. The other option was not acceptable to her.

Stone sighed and turned back to the fight. "Let's hope you're right, little Fae girl."

Moments later, Keegan was thrown across the arena. He skidded to a halt, and lay there on his side, breathing hard.

"Get up," Bitsy whispered. Pain in her palms made her flinch, and she looked down to find crescent-shaped beads of blood from her nails. When she raised her head again,

Merrick was standing over the limp form of the white wolf, teeth bared in a snarl.

"Let's go," Stone told them.

"It's not over yet," Bitsy protested.

"We need to go now," he told her. "While everyone is distracted."

"What about the others?" her father asked.

"I can't help them right now. We'll figure out something else."

He tried to pull her with him, but she'd be damned if she was going to go anywhere without Keegan. "Why don't you help him?" Her voice was high and laced with panic, but she couldn't help it. She glanced over at the two wolves. Merrick was pacing around his opponent, prodding him now and again with his nose or paw.

Keegan bared his teeth but seemed able to do little else.

She struck out at Stone with her fist. "Help him, you idiot!"

"That's not the way it goes," Stone bit out. "If I helped him, it would bring him more shame than just losing the fight."

"Fuck that!" she yelled. "He would be alive."

"Let's GO," he ordered.

"NO," she told him.

"Honey, there's nothing you can do," her father said.

Bitsy dug in her heels. She wasn't leaving. Not yet. And when she turned back to the fight, she let out a whoop.

Keegan was on his feet, head down, his front left paw held off the ground. The fur on his face was rusty with blood and dirt, but his green eyes glowed with purpose as they glared up at Merrick.

"It's not over. Look. Just look!" she insisted when Stone shook his head.

For a moment, she didn't think he would do it, but then he did. However, unlike her own reaction, his was grim. "It's as good as over. We have to go."

That was not an acceptable answer for her. Not after everything. Without warning, Bitsy ran right into the middle of the fight and launched herself onto Merrick's back. Weak from the iron surrounding her, she had no power, hardly any strength, but she had to try. Wrapping one arm around his furry neck, she cursed loudly in his ear as he growled, bucked, and twisted his body, trying to dislodge her. She managed to give him one good knock in the side of the head with the cuff around her wrist before someone grabbed her around the middle and she was torn away.

She landed on her ass in the dirt, but whoever interfered didn't have a chance to do anything more to her before a black wolf flew over her head and landed behind her. Twisting around, she found it on top of Gold Tooth with its teeth around his throat.

Stone.

A bit surprised the rest of the shifters didn't join in the melee, she turned back around to check on Keegan and found herself face to face with Merrick's snarling muzzle. But she wasn't afraid.

She was pissed off.

With a scream of rage, she struck out with a clenched fist and hit him square in the temple with the iron cuff. His grey head barely budged. Teeth, long and yellow, dripped with saliva two inches from her face.

Bitsy snarled right back at him. But then a hair-raising howl rent the air as Keegan threw his head back and howled, successfully drawing Merrick's attention away from her. Then he launched himself at his foe.

Hands beneath her arms dragged Bitsy out of the way as the two Alphas went at it again in a flurry of snapping teeth and flying fur.

"What the fuck are you doing? Your mother would never forgive me if she knew I'd allowed you to throw yourself into the middle of a wolf fight."

"Well, it worked for Bronaugh when she did it."

"Do we really need to get into a discussion about why that might be?"

Distracted by the fight, Bitsy just grabbed hold of her father's arm around her middle and held on tight. Keegan yelped as Merrick bit him hard on the shoulder, and Bitsy squeezed her eyes shut and hid her face in her father's shirt. When she opened them, she was looking at the she-wolf—Corrina.

The female was glaring at her, like it was her fault the boys were brawling again.

More like she just didn't like the fact they were fighting over her.

Narrowing her eyes, Bitsy flipped her off, loud and clear. Let the bitch stare at that.

Corrina suddenly whipped her head around, and her eyes went wide.

Bitsy followed the direction of her gaze and found the tide had shifted.

Keegan, the light colors of his fur nearly indistinguishable from all the blood and dirt, reared up on his hind legs and took Merrick down. The wolves rolled over and over, and for few seconds, it was hard to tell who had the upper hand.

But when they stopped, Keegan was on top.

An anguished scream came from the opposite side of the arena as he reared back, jaws open wide, and clamped them down on Merrick's throat. With a hard shake of his head, he tore through the fur and skin. Another shake and he came away with half of Merrick's throat in his mouth. He dropped the bloody mass on the ground, threw back his head, and howled in triumph.

He was joined by a chorus of others, some in wolf form and some still human.

Corrina's screams blended and harmonized with them, creating a song of death and grief and victory.

Keegan stumbled back and sank onto his haunches. His eyes found Bitsy, protected by Stone, and then they rolled back in his head as his body tumbled heavily to the ground.

And so did her heart.

"What the fuck were you doing?" Keegan demanded. They were the first words he'd spoken the entire ride back to the hotel. He'd been too furious up until now.

"Saving you, Asshat." Bitsy rolled her eyes.

Her attitude made him want to kiss her and yell at her all at the same time. Instead, he reached over the console of Stone's truck he'd borrowed and took her small hand in his. She was warm and alive and *there*. And so was he. "I'm coming up to your room."

"Damn right you are," she said under her breath, and laced her fingers tightly through his.

Keegan grinned, then winced and scowled. His face hurt. Actually, his entire body hurt, but not nearly as much as it had.

Challenging Merrick again before he'd had time to heal from the first scuffle was probably the most dumbass thing he'd ever done. In retrospect, he should have listened to Stone. His plan had been sound and would've given them all a better chance to get out of there alive.

But Keegan was no coward. And he wasn't about to just give up his home, his pack, and sneak away in the middle of the night with his tail tucked between his legs. He'd nearly lost, again, and he'd been prepared to do so if it would allow him to die an honorable death and give Stone the chance to get Bitsy out of that fucking arena and to safety.

Then Bitsy had attacked Merrick from behind, and all of that violence had been turned on her, and Keegan had lost his fucking mind.

He didn't even remember what all had happened after that. Just the coppery taste of blood as he spit Merrick's throat out of his mouth, and the sense of relief when he found Bitsy wrapped in her father's arms, Stone's furry black hide planted next to her. And then everything had gone dark.

The first time he came to, he was still in the arena, back in his human form, in agonizing pain, and surrounded by two packs of shifters. As soon as they saw he was awake, they shifted, exposing their throats in submission to their Alpha. Somehow, he'd managed to get to his feet, as the wolves yipped and howled to his victory.

Bitsy stayed back, her dark eyes shifting between him and the other wolves, silently taking in the whole process.

He tried to reach out to her but blacked out again.

The next time he woke, he was in his room, alone. A commotion outside roused him enough to try to get out of bed. Limping over to the window, he drew the curtain aside just in time to see the roof of the barn come crashing down. Panic sent him swaying on his feet, afraid Bitsy was still inside with the others, but then he spotted Stone down in the yard. His second in command turned and looked right up at him, as though he felt the weight of Keegan's stare. With a grin, he waved, took a bow, and went back to directing the demolition of the rodeo.

Needing to see what was happening for himself, Keegan hobbled over to his dresser to get some clothes. But one look in the mirror at his dirt and blood-coated body had him bee-lining for the shower. Stiff and aching, it took him longer than he wanted. But, eventually, he was clean and dressed.

Bareheaded, as his last hat was probably still inside the barn where he'd tossed it, he made his way down the stairs and out the back door. His heart pounded in his chest as another section of the barn came crashing down, sending waves of sharp pain through his temples.

"You're up."

Keegan swung around.

Bitsy sat alone on the porch swing, watching the destruction. When he just stood there staring at her, she stopped swinging and stood. "Keegan?"

For a few seconds, he could do nothing but blink.

She was wearing a long, flowy, green skirt with a sporty yellow tank, striped socks, and those ugly orange shoes. Her dark hair stuck out all over her head, and little lines creased the skin between her delicate eyebrows as she scowled at him. Her silver necklace gleamed in the sunlight, the pendant tucked between her full breasts.

"What's the matter with you? Should you be up?"

His relief swiftly turned to fury as the events of the

previous night crashed into his head. And along with the anger was fear. Fear something would as yet happen to her, even though she seemed to be doing just fine hanging out with the pack while he lay upstairs half-dying. Fear one of them would suddenly decide she didn't belong in their world. Fear they wouldn't tolerate her walking around free.

Without a word, he grabbed her by the hand and pulled her down the steps. "Stone!"

Stone turned, took in what was happening, reached into his front pocket, and threw Keegan a set of keys.

Keegan caught them mid-air and hit the button to unlock Stone's truck. He opened the passenger door for Bitsy and shoved her inside before climbing into the driver's seat. Tires spinning, he got the fuck out of there as fast as he could.

Bitsy tried to talk to him, tried to find out where they were going, but his teeth were clenched together so hard he couldn't answer her if he'd wanted to. He wasn't sure exactly what was happening, he was just following his instincts. And those instincts were telling him to get her out of that place and back to the hotel.

They were halfway to Austin before he calmed down enough to speak, but mostly he just held her hand.

He pulled up to the valet and threw the truck into park, leaving it running. "Do you have your room key?"

"Nope. Things like that tend to get lost when I'm being lassoed and hog-tied."

He ignored her snarky tone and changed direction, heading over to the front desk. In no time at all, they had two more keys and were climbing the stairs up to her room. Probably because the desk clerk was now scared to death of him, but Keegan didn't care. When Bitsy didn't move fast enough, he scooped her up into his arms, ignoring the pull of sore muscles, and didn't put her down again until they'd reached her door.

It took him two tries to get the key to work, but he finally got them both inside her lavish room. He locked the door and turned to find her right behind him.

Now that he had her alone, there was so much he wanted to say, but she beat him to it.

"I hated you."

"I know."

"You left me there. AGAIN."

"I did." There was no sense in making excuses.

The tight line of her mouth softened. "You came back for me."

"Of course I came back for you, ittybit." Keegan reached out and smoothed away the last of her frown with his thumb. "I'm sorry I wasn't there sooner. He told me he would kill you right in front of me if I didn't leave, and I took him at his word. Merrick wasn't one to fuck around. And I reckon the crowd would have backed him up. Even my own pack was on the fence about me, other than Stone. There was no way I could have gotten to you. No way I could have fought them all off—"

"Shut up."

"Bitsy, please." He needed to explain, to say it out loud.

"I said shut up," she told him. "And kiss me already."

"I'm still pissed off at you for throwing yourself into the middle of it."

She took a step closer, then another, until her breasts

were brushing his ribs. Her nipples hardened with every breath as her hands slid over his chest to grip his shoulders. "Are you going to fight with me? Or are you going to kiss me?"

He ran his hands down her ribcage and over the curves of her hips. Bending down, he lifted her and wrapped her legs around his waist, then pressed her back against the wall. "I thought we could do both."

Her heart thudded against his chest. It matched the racing of his own. Neither of them made a move as they studied each other. They barely breathed.

"I hated you," she finally whispered.

Keegan saw the emotion in her eyes. It was the same for him. "You had every right to." He lowered his head until his mouth was barely an inch from her own and he could feel her warm, sweet breath fan his face. "Do you still hate me, ittybit?"

Tears filled her eyes. "No."

"That's good, because I'm not leaving you anywhere again."

"How do I know I can trust you?"

"Other than the fact that I just nearly died for you?"

A smile teased the edges of her mouth. "Yes. Other than that."

"You're just gonna have to take my word for it."

He closed the remaining distance between them. Her lips were soft and warm and trembling with a vulnerability she would never admit to, and he would never dare to mention. Her hands cupped his face as he kissed her, slowly at first, taking his time, even though his body shuddered with need. But soon, the heat flared between them, as it always did.

One hand under her bottom, he slid the other beneath her skirt, up her smooth calf to her curvy thigh, and higher. She wore absolutely nothing beneath the skirt, and Keegan growled deep in his throat as her sweet ass filled his palm.

Keegan backed away from the wall and tucked her head to his shoulder. Striding to her room, he gently lowered her to the bed. But he didn't fall on her right away, because the sight of her lying there—fully clothed but open and welcoming, with no shame in her eyes or conflict in her expression or body—momentarily took his breath away.

Still staring, he kicked off his boots and took his shirt off, enjoying the way her eyes roamed over his chest and arms like he was a feast to be consumed.

She reached for him, and he quickly rid himself of his jeans and joined her on the bed. Her hands were everywhere. They ran up his arms, squeezing his biceps before traveling up to his shoulders and down his back as far as she could reach. She kissed the side of his neck, her breath chilling that same spot a moment later. With a groan, he rolled his hips into her soft belly, and she opened her legs for him as she nipped his shoulder.

"Ittybit..." His arms shook as he tried not to crush her, and he softly cursed his healing body.

Suddenly, he was flipped onto his back, and he grunted at the pain. But it was soon forgotten as Bitsy pulled her skirt out of the way and straddled his hips. His breath caught as she pulled her tank up and off, exposing her full breasts to his hungry gaze. He caught one in his hand, and her hardened nipple grazed his palm.

Bitsy's head fell back as she arched her spine, her nails digging into his stomach and her hips rocking over him. His length slid between her legs, against her wet core, and she moaned as he hit the little bundle of nerves.

That sound alone nearly made him come all over his stomach.

Keegan grasped the waistline of her skirt and yanked until the thin material gave way. He tugged it out from under her legs and tossed it to the floor. Hands on her hips, he lifted her, bringing her to his mouth. Bitsy cried out with the first touch of his tongue, spreading her knees on each side of his head as he found her with his fingers and thrust inside.

Her body tightened above him, hovered there, and then she cried out his name as she fell apart. Her body bucked forward, and she braced her hands against the headboard. Her heavy breasts swayed above his eyes, and he wrapped his arms around the tops of her thighs and held her tight to his mouth as she shuddered over and over.

When he finally released her, he was aching all over in an entirely different way. His skin felt too hot, his balls were tight, and his cock was painfully hard.

Bitsy scooted down his body and he lifted his hips, meeting her halfway. He felt her heat with the tip of his cock, and with one powerful thrust, he slid inside her tight body. Taking her beautiful face between his palms, he kissed her, swallowing her cries as he rocked his hips.

When he was fully sheathed inside of her, he gripped

her hip with one hand, holding her still. Keegan kissed her gently and thoroughly, losing himself in the taste of her, in the feel of her.

She pulled back, and their eyes locked. "Keegan…" She stopped, biting her lower lip.

Though he ached for the words he saw reflected in her dark eyes, he would wait until she was ready to say them. It would take time, he knew. And that was okay. They had all the time in the world. "I know, ittybit."

Drawing her lips back to his, he rolled his hips.

She moaned, and began to rock, sliding his cock almost all the way out before she took him in again.

Keegan groaned as his balls pulled up even tighter, his orgasm teasing him. Bending his legs, he took over, sinking into her willing body faster and faster. He pulled her tight to his chest, her pendant warm on his skin, holding her close as his orgasm seized him and his cries joined hers. Then he started all over again.

He left the ugly orange shoes on. Because they made her happy.

And he wanted nothing more than to make her happy.

For the rest of their lives.

✳ ✳ ✳

Thank you for reading! I hope you loved Keegan and Bitsy's story. The next book in The Kincaid Werewolves series is
<u>A Wolf's Promise.</u>
Lucian has always been the hothead of the group. Find out if he can be tamed when he meets Keelin…

<u>READ A WOLF'S PROMISE NOW</u>

"FANFREAKINTASTIC!! I absolutely LOVED this book!! I have been waiting for Lucian's story for what seems like forever and it was soooo worth the wait!!"
- Amazon Review

"I loved this book, I read it in one sitting. This author is in my top 10 of favourite authors, she knows how to write a brilliant story." -Amazon review

L.E. Wilson writes Paranormal Romance starring intense alpha males and the women who are fearless enough to tame them — for the most part anyway. ;) In her novels you'll find smoking hot scenes, a touch of suspense, some humor, a bit of gore, and multifaceted characters, all working together to combine her lifelong obsession with the paranormal and her love of romance.

Her writing career came about the usual way: on a dare from her loving husband. Little did she know just one casual suggestion would open a box of worms (or words as the case may be) that would forever change her life.

Peach tea and her tiara are a necessary part of her writing process, though sometimes you'll find her typing away at her favorite Starbucks. She walks two miles to get there, to make up for all of those coffees. On the weekends she likes to hike, garden, cook vegan food, and have date nights with her favorite guy.

On a Personal Note:
"I love to hear from my readers! Contact me anytime at le@lewilsonauthor.com."

Keep In Touch With L.E.
lewilsonauthor.com
le@lewilsonauthor.com

www.ingramcontent.com/pod-product-compliance
Lightning Source LLC
Chambersburg PA
CBHW021136190726
48288CB00008B/2684